B52 005

KT-231-197

TOWER OF ROCKS

A Western Duo

Steve Frazee

CHIVERS

British Library Cataloguing in Publication Data available

This Large Print edition published by AudioGO Ltd, Bath, 2013.
Published by arrangement with Golden West Literary Agency

U.K. Hardcover   ISBN   978 1 4713 2674 5
U.K. Softcover   ISBN   978 1 4713 2675 2

Copyright © 2005 by Eric Frazee

'Death Rides This Trail!' by Steve Frazee first appeared in Western Story Magazine (10/53). Copyright © 1953 by Popular Publications, Inc. Copyright © renewed 1981 by Steve Frazee. Copyright © 2004 by Eric Frazee for restored material.

All rights reserved

ROTHERHAM LIBRARY &
INFORMATION SERVICES

B 52005613 8

Printed and bound in Great Britain by
TJ International Limited

TABLE OF CONTENTS

DEATH RIDES THIS TRAIL!

I

A few days after they saw the two wagoneers slicing each other raw with bull whips, the Breslins broke out of the sandy country and saw a wild sweep of hills humping across the horizon. They were in bright sunshine but up ahead a storm, black and sudden, was knotting itself to lash out.

Dirk Breslin reined old Put closer to the wagon. The oncoming storm, rushing up so suddenly in the great space all around him, made him uneasy. There seemed to be no limit or plan to anything out here. His sixteen years had been spent on a farm in settled country, where trees and fields, the river, and painted buildings marked the boundaries of a safe, familiar world.

With a touch of envy he glanced to the left, where his brother Hugh was riding far on the flank, looking for buffalo. Hugh was a year younger than Dirk. His worn-out old

7

rifle wouldn't kill a buffalo if he saw one, but Hugh was out there trying. It took a lot to discourage Hugh or scare him out.

On the wagon beside his wife, Jake Breslin raised a long arm. "That's it, Em," he said. "About a hundred and fifty miles yonder of those hills."

The four younger kids scrambled forward in the wagon to peer ahead, as if they thought they could put their eyes on their new home.

Talbot said: "Where, Pa? I don't see nothing but a lot of land."

Pa said: "You'll see when we get there."

The storm was boiling toward them now. Dirk pulled a little closer to the wagon. Back home there was always a place to run when a storm came, into the big barn, or under a walnut tree.

Ma tied her bonnet strings. "Sometimes I think this is a brutal land, Jake. I know it's a violent land."

Jake laughed. "You're still thinking of those wagon drivers, Em. Sure, its rough out here, so you have to get just as rough as the country to lick it."

Ma Breslin looked at the heavy pistol in her husband's waistband. He had never carried one before; there was no cause to do so where the Breslins came from. But Jake had observed the custom of the country and now he was armed.

Wind and dust whirled against them first, and then the rain struck furiously. Ma pushed the kids back under the canvas top and lashed the strings. Pa began to sing, with the water bouncing on his broad face.

Huddled on old Put, feeling the cold seeping against flesh that had been too hot minutes before, Dirk took courage from his father. The rain washing harmlessly against the brown, clean-shaven planes of Pa's face reminded Dirk of a picture in his grandmother's parlor back home — a violent sea lashing up at unyielding rock. In the distance, Hugh went on with his futile hunt, paying no attention to the rain.

It had taken Dirk a long time to realize that each member of the family was utterly different from the others. Missouri, his oldest sister, was sharp-tongued at times — the rest of the time she was inclined to lightness and song. Pa said she was just like Ma had been when she was a little younger. Talbot, who was a twin to Cree, the other sister, was quiet, always tinkering with things, claiming he could build things better than the way they already were. He didn't talk much, and some folks thought he wasn't quite smart because of that. Lafayette, the youngest, was a crybaby, never wanting to fight even when he was picked on. Dirk considered them all. He wished he himself had more of Pa's strong nature — because he was afraid he was exactly like Lafayette.

The storm swept away, leaving a clean odor of silky dust caught in the air, and the land all wet and steaming around them. The vastness still caught at Dirk's stomach, but he kept watching Pa — he knew the country wouldn't be too mean for Pa to handle. Hugh was clean out of sight now.

Four days later the hills were close ahead, green billows tumbling one upon another. The Breslins came to a muddy river and there was a camp of sorts in a grove of cottonwoods, with wagons scattered here and there, with horses held in a rope corral, the first Dirk had ever seen.

"That tent's a saloon," Ma said. "I can tell from here. Don't you stay in there no longer than necessary to get directions, Jake Breslin."

Pa grinned. "Out here most of the talking and business is done in saloons, Em. Have Dirk take the wagon on to the river and water the horses. I'll be along."

Big and confident, with a pistol in his

waistband, Pa went into the tent. When Dirk drove by, he heard the clink of glasses and his father laughing, already getting acquainted. Men liked Jake Breslin. Dirk was proud of that.

Dirk went on toward the racing water. The trees and the river were not the same as back home, but they still made Dirk like the country a little better. Down here distances were sort of shut away. He hoped their new home in the Topknot country would be sheltered.

He and Hugh watered the team. The shots came when the younger ones were wading in the cool mud. They were cracking little sounds, not like the heavy gushing of rifles or the roar of big pistols.

Hugh ran to the wagon and grabbed his rifle. He went through the trees toward the saloon.

"Hugh!" Ma called, but he did not stop. "Go after him, Dirk!" she said. All at once her face was white.

Dirk overtook his brother just before they reached the tent. There was a crowd of men in front, and women coming from all directions.

"You had no call for that," a man was saying. "You could see he wasn't after a pistol fight."

"He wore a gun, Coupland. When a damned Yankee shoots off his mouth to me, and he's wearing a pistol, he gets what he asks for."

"There was no call for it. If we had any law out here. . . . Wait a minute, there, son!"

Hugh had thrust his way deeply into the crowd, with Dirk right behind him. Pa was lying on the ground. His feet were spraddled out all funny-like. There was dust on the clean tan of one cheek. His eyes were wide open. Dirk had never seen a dead person except in the church back home, but he knew Pa was dead.

Hugh was raising his rifle toward a tall, dark-faced man with a trim mustache. The man was holding a tiny little pistol without a trigger guard. Hugh didn't say anything. His blond hair was hanging on his forehead. His blue eyes had turned pale. He cocked the rifle as he raised it. The man called Coupland, gray-haired and almost fat, grabbed the barrel and jerked it up and Hugh's shot went toward a clear sky. He began to struggle for the weapon, not cursing, not saying anything.

"You should have let him, Judge," a man said. He stepped toward the dark man with the tiny gun. "Boys, I say let's string this one up right now!"

"No!" Judge Coupland cried. He was holding Hugh in his arms, trying to smother the fight out of him without hurting him. Another man helped him, and then Hugh began to cry.

Ma Breslin came in then. The crowd parted, men taking off their hats. Ma was a handsome woman, with dark-brown hair and eyes to look through a man. Even now, white with shock, she was tall and steady as she went to Jake. Dirk didn't want to go. The strangeness of his father was a searing pain inside. But he did go over, and a moment later was kneeling there with Hugh, and both of them were crying.

He heard Coupland say: "It's a shame there's no law here, but we can't take it into our hands. I'll swallow my scruples, however, and provide the rope, if you're not gone from here in five minutes."

"It wouldn't be advisable for farmers to try to hang me, my friend." The man who had killed Pa held a big pistol in his hand now. There was white at the collar of his dark coat. The hand on the pistol was long and slender. Those two facts impressed themselves on Dirk's mind, and he knew he would forever hold a grudge against any man with soft hands or who wore a white shirt. The man backed away, still holding

13

the pistol. "Ah, well," he said, "this place was about worked out anyway." Dirk Breslin was never to see him again.

They buried Jacob Breslin that afternoon.

Lafayette continued to cry long after there was no visible reason for grief. Dirk slapped him, hating him at the moment, for Dirk himself wanted to bawl, and there was no relief in it. He knew just how Lafayette felt, and slapped him because it seemed to be a blow at his own weakness. He was sorry when it was done. He wanted to say so, but Lafayette walked away from him, his face all streaked with dust and tears, no longer crying.

That night all the women from the wagons that were waiting for the river to go down came to the Breslin fire with gifts of food that no one but Talbot had appetite to touch. Stolid Talbot stuffed himself.

Dirk and Hugh slipped away with their father's pistol. It was an old one, with the butt grips cracked and loose. They sat together under a dark cottonwood close to the growling water, passing the pistol between them.

"There's customs out here, huh?" Dirk said. "We'll get us another pistol just like this one, Hugh."

"Maybe we won't stay here that long. I

guess we'll be going back home now."

They had no home to go to. It was hundreds of miles back to where they had sold the farm, and still a hundred to where Jake Breslin had intended to go. Alone in the night, beside the rushing water, the two boys fondled the pistol, and suddenly there was no courage in it.

"I'm sort of scared . . . a little," Hugh said. "It was all right with Pa, but now I'm sort of scared. . . ."

It was one of the few times Hugh ever admitted being afraid of anything.

"I guess we'll go back now, huh, Dirk? Back to Ma's folks?"

When there was action at hand, Hugh never asked anyone's advice; he acted. Dirk began to understand. Leadership was being nudged toward him now that Pa was gone, because Hugh didn't like to look beyond the next move, or maybe he couldn't.

"We won't go back," Dirk said. "We're going on to where Pa wanted to go. We got to do that now." He was frightened a moment later by his statement, but it was out.

"All right, Dirk. I guess you're the boss now."

Hugh was satisfied. Worn out with grief and travel, he fell asleep soon afterward, resting his head on Dirk's shoulder. Dirk could not fall asleep so easily. He sat there, thinking of the quiet orchards along the river back home, and of tagging along behind Grandfather Sterns when the old man went out to inspect the apples. He thought then of the stark space of all the country around him, and he saw his father on the ground in front of a faded tent, with dust on his cheek and his eyes wide open.

The pistol on Dirk's lap took coldness from the night. Hugh whimpered in his sleep. Dirk sat there with the tears hot against his twisted cheeks until his mother's voice, calling him, came faintly from the camp.

After breakfast the next morning, Emma Breslin said they would start the long trip back. Dirk's resolution had faded with the night. He started to speak and then thought better of it. After all, now that Pa was gone. . . .

Hugh said: "No, Ma, Dirk said we were going on, just like Pa would want us to."

With her lips firm and the trouble in her as real as something that can be felt, Dirk's mother bore a long study on him. "You want to go on, Dirk?"

He nodded, unsure of words. Talbot stared at him with admiration. Lafayette began to cry. He wanted to go home, he said. Missouri, Dirk's oldest sister, dark and slender like her mother, shook her head at Dirk.

"He's scared, Ma. I can tell. He says go on just to show off."

"He ain't scared!" Hugh said. "You just wait until the river makes the wagon float and the horses have to swim, and then you'll see who's scared."

"That's enough," Emma Breslin said. "I guess we'd all better talk about this some more. You might be right, Dirk, but I haven't the courage myself to go on."

It was Hugh who pushed Dirk into swinging the final decision to go on into Topknot country. Dirk knew it, but Hugh did not.

Rumor had it that Judge Coupland had come West for his health. Except for a certain paleness of complexion that the sun did not seem to change, he did not look like a health seeker. He rode into the Breslin camp when the wagons were at the river and getting ready to cross. Although his hair was iron gray, there was an unlined look of youthfulness on his features. His forehead was broad, his chin narrow and blunt. When he spoke, he had a habit of pushing out his thick lips as if giving a mild judicial opinion. If Dirk had not seen him speak with fire in his eyes to the gambler who had killed Jake

Breslin, Dirk would have taken Coupland for an utterly harmless man.

The judge — a term of honor only, since he was a lawyer and there was no law — peered mildly at the two large cottonwood logs Dirk and Hugh had skidded in to lash to the wagon. "Do you mean, Missus Breslin, that you're going on?"

"We are. The older boys have changed my decision of last night."

"I see . . . I see." Coupland looked at Dirk appraisingly. "I applaud your decision, madam, although my personal opinion is that the Topknot country is unsuited for farming."

"What's wrong with it?" Mrs. Breslin asked.

"A lack of water, mainly, from what my information tells me. The soil, I understand, is quite productive, but there are only two small streams out there." Coupland looked dubiously at the gathering wagons. "So many people in one small area, with but two sources of water. The rains out there, I understand, are not dependable."

"He's probably going there himself," Hugh muttered.

Two snub-nosed boys in butternut jeans and boots they were obviously proud of, since they had rolled their pants legs high to expose the leather, came close to the Breslin wagon and stood there, grinning insolently as they looked at the logs, and then at Dirk and Hugh.

Judge Coupland swung down from his Kentucky horse and talked to Emma Breslin. "I wouldn't tell this to everybody, madam, but it is my considered opinion that the country this side of the Topknot, the Breakwagon Hills, is admirably suited for raising cattle. Now if I had a family of sturdy sons. . . ."

"We know nothing of cattle, Mister Coupland. If we did, we lack the money to buy them."

"Most likely all these people will rush right on past the Breakwagon Hills, Missus Breslin. I strongly recommend you stop and consider what I've said when you reach that part of the country."

Dirk didn't know whether or not to trust Coupland. The idea of being a cattle rancher was appealing, but the Breslins had only a few hundred dollars. That wouldn't buy enough cattle to stick in your eye, Dirk surmised, thinking in terms of the huge milch cows back home.

One of the boys in butternut jeans said to Hugh: "Do you know how to get across this river?" It was insolent. The boy was quite sure Hugh didn't know.

Hugh bristled. "Huh, I guess we do. We'll get someone to help us lift these here logs up so we can tie 'em against the wagon and then. . . ."

The two boys laughed, nudging each other. Their hair was long against the collars of their shirts. Their eyes, bold green, were as insolent as their laughs.

"They're going to lift the logs up and hold 'em there to be tied, Tommy! I told you they didn't know nothing. Look at them bare feet."

Hugh dug his toes against the ground. He grinned. "I know something," he said, walking forward.

"Yeah," Tommy said suspiciously, "what?"

Hugh grabbed Tommy, tripped him off balance, spun him across his hip, and then sent him rolling into the water at the edge of the river. He reached for the second smart aleck. The second boy began to hammer Hugh in the face. Hugh kept walking in, reaching out, but his opponent was handy with his fists and bigger than Hugh. Hugh's nose began to bleed. Red marks blossomed on his cheeks. He kept coming in.

Tommy was getting out of the river.

"Get the other one, Hugh!" Dirk wound

up a swing and hit Hugh's adversary in the side of the jaw so hard he knocked him over one of the dead logs.

Hugh let out a yell. He went back and threw his first opponent into the river again. They wrestled there, rolling in the mud and water.

Ma Breslin was calling out to Hugh and Dirk. Hugh never would have heard, and Dirk couldn't let go if he wanted to. He was getting more than he bargained for from the heavier boy. Dirk swung with all his might, but he wasn't hitting anything, and hard knuckles were bouncing off his face every second or two. He lowered his head and butted the boy in the stomach. That helped. They went over the log together, and then Dirk got his hands in his opponent's long hair and began to pound the boy's head against the ground.

The kid hooked his thumbs under the corner of Dirk's lips and dug his fingers in behind Dirk's ears. Dirk couldn't bite the thumbs. He thought his mouth was being stretched four feet wide. All he could do was keep beating the boy's head against the ground, and the ground was soft.

Judge Coupland hauled Dirk off by the suspenders. The boy held on with his thumbs until Dirk smacked him in the nose.

"What a country," Coupland murmured. "The children start in like wildcats the minute they get here."

There was a crowd of men around now, grinning. A worried-looking little fellow with a meager beard was holding Tommy. Beside the man was a ponderous woman with hair in a tight knot at the back of her head.

"Fighting, fighting," she said. "I swear, Bolivar, all these young 'uns have done since we started. . . ."

"I'll learn you, Tommy!" Bolivar said. He slapped the boy so hard he lost his grip and knocked the lad into the water again.

"They started it!" Dirk said. "They . . . !"

Something popped on his cheek. He blinked. He saw a pair of blazing green eyes and two pigtails bouncing. A girl about his own age hauled off and smacked him three or four more times in the face. "You're a big bully!" she cried. She broke away then, and started to run, and wound up in the grip of the huge woman who had been at the edge of the water a few moments before.

"Callie, you ain't no lady a-tall," the woman said. She held the girl with one hand and spanked her where it hurt. "You're worse'n the boys sometimes, I do think, Callie."

The woman came waddling on to Mrs. Breslin. "Brats do beat all, don't they, Missus Breslin? I was telling my Bolivar just the other night that what Tommy and Squire" — she pronounced it Square — "and Callie need is a few Indians to scare the pants offen them."

"It's a violent land, Missus Bascomb," Ma Breslin said. "I have found that out."

"I know, you poor thing. You come over to the wagon, Missus Breslin. Bolivar ain't going across until we see how the river handles the other wagons. You and me will have some tea."

She gave Squire a mighty jerk by the arm. "You git, and stay out of trouble!"

Squire managed to dig his elbow, hard, into Dirk's ribs as he went by. Dirk tried to trip him, but the boy skipped away. He looked back insolently, unbeaten. The two of them right then knew they would never like each other.

Bolivar Bascomb was coming from the river. He made an open-handed pass at his son. Squire ducked and Bolivar went on around with the blow and nearly fell. "I'm right sorry about this, Missus Breslin, considering the trouble you've had already." Bolivar shook his head. He was an ineffectual-looking little man, and he seemed to be wondering how he had come by sons with so much fire in them.

"It's all right, Mister Bascomb," Ma Breslin said.

Judge Coupland wiped his brow. The first wagon was getting ready to try the crossing. He looked at the muddy surge of the rain-swelled river and appeared relieved to think that the next obstacle would be a natural one.

Hugh and Dirk drew together. "I guess we showed them," Hugh said.

Dirk felt his cheek. "Look at Missouri and Cree!"

The Breslin girls were chatting friendly-like to Callie. Ma Breslin and Mrs. Bascomb walked away together toward the Bascomb wagon.

Women . . . you just didn't know what they would do, Dirk thought. "I should have smacked that Callie girl," he grumbled.

Hugh grinned. "I'd 'a' rassled with her, if she'd slapped me. She's a kind of pretty girl, Dirk."

"You're too damned young to be talking like that!"

Hugh felt his swollen nose and grinned again. "Yeah, and you're too young to be cussing like that, too."

The first wagon went into the river. Dirk

saw then why the Bascomb boys had laughed at him and Hugh. The men didn't try to lift the heavy logs. They just put the wagon in deep enough so they could float the logs against it and tie them without any hard work at all. There were a lot of things you had to learn fast in this country. Dirk would learn them as fast as he could, and keep his mouth shut hereafter when he didn't know.

II

The first wagon inched out into the flood with the driver swearing at the horses when they tried to buckle around and get back to shore. Then the team was swimming. The dirty water came up until the logs were half submerged, and the current quartered the wagon downstream. Kids were peering out of the back of it, laughing.

Good Lord! Dirk was scared. Those kids ought to stay back where they couldn't fall out. It was only a quarter of a mile across, but Dirk lived a long time before he saw the dripping horses coming clear of the water on the far shore. A spare team that had been swum across earlier was there to help the wagon up the bank.

"That looks like a lot of fun," Hugh said. "Can I drive when we go across?"

"No. I can handle the team better." Dirk doubted that, but it was best he drive himself because he knew how scared he was.

When it was time for the Breslin wagon to go, Dirk found no joy in the confidence his mother placed in him. A man helped Hugh and Dirk start the extra team across by themselves, and a rider swam his horse behind them in case they tried to turn back in midstream.

Lafayette began to cry when the first hard clutch of the river swung the wagon at an angle. "Don't fret," Ma said. "Dirk will get us across just like the others."

"He'll more'n likely drown us all," Missouri said from inside the wagon. "If he does, I'll. . . ."

Hugh laughed. "What can you do, all swelled up like them dead buffalo we saw on the Missouri?"

"Hugh!" Ma called. "You keep your mouth shut!"

The current was a mighty hand that made the wagon tremble. It was a long way to either shore now. The waves were slobbering foam that slapped over the backs of the swimming horses. Dirk kept gulping fear. He tried to talk cheerfully to the team, like Pa used to do. Pa was gone forever now, back there on the hill above a place that

26

didn't even have a name. Dirk wanted to give way a little, but he held the lines loosely and kept talking to the horses.

"It's wet in here!" Missouri cried. "We're sinking!"

"We ain't, either!" Hugh laughed again.

The far shore came to them and they landed right where the other wagons had struck. A red-faced man backed a team of grays down to help them up the bank, after Hugh unlashed the logs. The man saw nothing unusual in the crossing.

Dirk felt better, but there was a hardness in his stomach yet. He looked back. The Bascombs were just ready to start. Mrs. Bascomb waved. Bolivar held the lines. Hah, that Squire couldn't talk about driving the river when he came across.

"Next time, maybe, I'll let Hugh have the fun," Dirk said.

"There are no more rivers like this between here and the Topknot country, thank the Lord." Ma hugged Lafayette. He wasn't crying now.

It became a race the second day away from the river, when the wagons hit the first of the rolling hills. There was free land on the Topknot and some, of course, would be better than other. On the third day the wagons were no longer camping together.

The Breslins and the Bascombs were behind. Dirk remembered well how Pa had cautioned about a shaky rear wheel, saying that he might have to stop and cut the rim down before getting to where they were going. The wheels were tight enough the first day away from the river, but the wood shrank quickly. Dirk took it easy.

Bolivar Bascomb's horses were old and poor. They could not rush. So the two groups stayed together. Missouri and Cree were right friendly with Callie, and Talbot and Lafayette sometimes talked to the Bascomb boys. Hugh and Dirk wanted no part of them.

Ma told Mrs. Bascomb and Bolivar what Judge Coupland had said about the Breakwagon Hills.

"Cattle are all right, I guess," Bolivar said. His big eyes rolled in wrinkled flesh. "If a body knew something about cattle and had the money and all. . . ." He looked at his hands. "I've always been a farmer, on a hillside place." Not a very good farmer, either, his attitude implied.

Dirk sort of liked Bolivar Bascomb. The name fascinated him, to begin with, and Bolivar wasn't mean in any way, just always worried.

The hills grew worse as they went on,

short chops of grassy ground that put a strain on everything. Sometimes there were wide-open spaces where the grass was high. There were tiny springs everywhere and spots of marshy ground. It looked all right for cattle, sure enough. All the other wagons had gone right on through.

On the fourth day Bolivar said: "There's no use holding you folks back." It had taken both teams to get the wagons up the worst of the hills, with everybody pushing. The Bascomb horses were about done. "I heard at the river place there was an easy way around these hills," Bolivar said. "You go north about fifteen miles. I guess that's what we'll do. No use holding you folks up no more."

Ma said it was all right, they didn't mind, and Dirk said so, too, but Bolivar shook his head. "We'll just mosey around the easy way, maybe give the team a few days' rest, and we'll see you on the Topknot."

The way the girls took on at parting you would have thought the Bascombs were going to China. Dirk shook Bolivar's hand. It sort of embarrassed him, but it also gave him the feel of being a grown-up man.

The hill was one of the worst. Dirk thought he should have brought some logs from the last grove of trees to sprag the wheels if the wagon started to slide back. But it was too late now. Lafayette was driving. He was the lightest. All he had to do was hold the lines. He was scared, ready to blubber, but he was doing his job.

Dirk was on old Put, and Hugh was riding the other saddle horse, Mitch. They had ropes on the wagon and were helping all they could. Ma and the rest were pushing. The grass was darned good and slick, and the shoes on Vicksburg and Island Ten were worn smooth. Pa had given the matched grays their names, after two places where he'd fought, but the names were just Vick and Ten now.

"All together!" Dirk shouted.

Vick and Ten clawed away and heaved. The hot sun rippled on their muscles and the sweat odor of them came up to Dirk.

The smaller front wheels were almost on the crest. Vick stumbled and lost all the motion. "Come on, Vick!" Lafayette cried in a trembling voice. The wagon began to slip. Vick recovered and did his best along with Ten. The other horses tried to hold, but all their efforts came to was keeping the wagon from smashing up when it finally slid to the bottom of the hill. The girls were red-faced and tired. Lather was dripping from the sides of the team.

"Let's unhitch the horses and rest a while right here," Mrs. Breslin panted. "Then we'll go up."

"This isn't the right hill," Missouri said.

"It is, too! You can see where the other wagons went up," Dirk said. "You're so smart, why don't you find a better hill, Misery."

"Don't you call me that! I'll slap you worse than Callie Bascomb did!"

"Come on, you wildcats," Ma said patiently. "We'll find a spring and eat, and then we'll feel better."

Hugh and Dirk unhitched the team and let the horses cool before they led them to a spring to drink.

"That back wheel is about gone," Dirk said. "The rim is sliding on it, almost."

"How you going to fix it?"

"After we get up the hill, we'll fix it." Some way. They could drive wooden wedges under the tire, and then it might hold till they reached the Topknot. It would be pretty bad if the Bascombs beat them, after all.

They felt better after eating. Missouri and Cree went up on a hill and picked flowers. "This is an awful pretty place right here," Missouri said when they returned. "There's some trees over there a ways. Why don't we just have our farm right here?"

"It would take twenty horses to get a plow through that sod," Ma said. "Especially an old bull plow like we have."

Dirk hadn't known that his mother knew the difference between a bull plow and a good one. He felt better about the task ahead. They would make it all right. Days of hard work and worrying about how to get the wagon on the next mile or two had left Dirk little time for the disturbing memory of his father on the ground before the tent. Only at night was he troubled; he guessed the vision would haunt him the rest of his life. But maybe after they did what Pa had wanted to do, he would feel easier about it.

"All of us at once now!" he called. The rest had done the team good. They came stoutly up the hill with Hugh and Dirk, dismounted this time, urging Put and Mitch to a steady pressure on the helping ropes.

Dirk saw the break coming where his rope began to unlay its yellow strands. He yelled for his mother and the others to get away from the wagon. The rope snapped on Vick's side of the wagon. It was not too great a jar, just enough to throw the horses off their stride. Lafayette might have urged them on up at the critical instant, but he was too slow, and his hands were tiny. Vick faltered with the front wheels just touching the crest. Motion stopped and the wagon then began to slide. Ten sensed the inexperience on the lines. He backed up. Then the horses and all went crashing back down the hill, with Hugh still fighting to keep strain on his rope.

The front wheels cramped around at the bottom. The weak rear wheel sent oak splinters flying when it cracked. Hugh was the first to the struggling horses. They were down and the wagon was on its side, with one broken corner of Ma's cherry-wood bureau showing through ripped canvas.

Ma and Dirk ran to where Lafayette had been thrown head over heels. For an instant Dirk thought he was dying, but it was only that the wind had been knocked from him. They pounded him on the back.

With his first breath Lafayette asked: "Who got hurt?"

"The wagon, is all." Dirk went over to help Hugh get the horses untangled. Ten stepped on Hugh's foot. Hugh cursed just like Pa had cursed now and then.

Ma didn't hear. She was leaning against the wagon, running her hand over the broken bureau.

"It's all right, Ma," Talbot said. "Maybe I can fix it."

Holding Cree's hand, Missouri said: "It ain't just busted bureaus and things like that, you . . . fool." She put her arm around her mother. For a while Dirk thought his mother was going to cry, but she blinked and smiled, and then gave the girls a hug.

"The wheel is darned good and busted," Talbot said. "You think we can fix it, Dirk?"

At the moment Dirk doubted the wagon wheel could ever be repaired, at least not well enough to stand any real heavy jolting. The last part of the trip, across the mountains, was the worst, Pa had said.

They were all watching Dirk when he straightened up from the wheel. "There was a blacksmith at the place where we crossed. He had a forge fixed up near the river and was doing some work. After a little while, maybe I'll ride back there. . . ."

"That big red-headed man with all the girls?" Talbot shook his head. "He went on with the others. His wagon was the second one across the river."

Dirk remembered now. He was all mixed up between yesterdays and now, and where they had been and where they were trying to go. He was tired and hot. He thought of the cool orchards on Grandfather Sterns's place back home.

"We got to unload the wagon, first thing," he said.

"Yeah, we should have before. . . ." Missouri stopped. She was sharp-tongued and critical, but, when there was bad trouble, she always did her part.

They piled their possessions on the grass — clothing, bedding, a few pieces of furniture, dishes, and tools. They really didn't have very much to fight this country with, Dirk thought. The feel of the vastness all around him came back with frightening oppressiveness. What they ought to do was turn right around and find some way to get back home.

Talbot got the big wrench and started loosening the wheels on the side that was up.

"What are you doing?" Dirk asked.

Talbot had thought it out, but he never could explain with words very well. His idea, when he finally got it out, was to remove the wheels and put skids under the wagon so the horse could drag it on up to a level place. Hugh took an axe and rode on to find trees for skids and pry poles to turn the wagon right side up. All of them together couldn't turn it. Talbot started to dig around the broken wheel.

"What's that for?" Dirk asked.

"We got to dig under the wheels, so we have a hole big enough to get at the nuts." Some folks thought Talbot was slow because he wasn't much to talk. Around strangers he didn't talk at all.

The shovels slipped and skidded on the grass. Underneath were root masses two feet deep, twined and intertwined. They grubbed with hoes and hacked with the edges of shovels. Ma was right about this being a country where it would take twenty horses to pull the plow. They burrowed under the hubs. Dirk lay on his back, with dirt and roots dropping in his face. He finally got the hub nuts off.

It was simple then to tip the wagon over in its skids. Sunset was with them when the horses pulled the box up the hill. They carried up their possessions and loaded them inside. A half mile ahead stood the grove of cottonwoods where Hugh had got the skids. Pulling steadily on the slick grass of level ground, Vick and Ten took the wagon to the trees, and there they stopped of their own accord, as if they knew their destination. The biggest spring the family had seen so far lay in the middle of the grove.

With the backwash of sunset crimson on the choppy hills around this plateau the Breslins sat wearily on the ground, too beaten at the moment to think of a fire and supper.

"Breakwagon Hills, they sure named 'em right," Hugh said.

Lafayette giggled, and then they were all laughing together. When it was over, Dirk wondered what kind of meanness there was in him to make him slap Lafayette when he was scared and crying.

Ma got up. "Build a fire, Talbot," she said.

She cooked an extra special supper that night. Afterward, around the fire, she led them in their evening hymn. There was a beauty in the words and tune that Dirk had never noticed before. He would look back years later and remember this night as one of the happiest times in the Breslins' lives. He fell asleep sitting on a log.

They had no intention of staying where they were. For three days the older boys worked to fashion wheel spokes with a drawknife from one of the heavy oaken sideboards of the wagon. Their hands were sore and festering with the bitter bite of splinters, but they were slowly making headway. And then the red-headed black-smith came back from the Topknot with his family. Josh Burrage was his name. His seven girls were all named after women of the Bible. He looked at the Breslins' handi-work.

"You boys have done right good there, but I misdoubt anything but a new wheel will cure your trouble. I had two spares when I passed here, but I sold one and then I busted a wheel and had to use the last one myself. I'm going back to the river place now. The Topknot country is crowded bad. Folks came in from the north way long before we got there. There's just a couple of little cricks and not near enough land to go around."

Burrage stayed two days. At the end of that time the Breslins' broken wheel was rebuilt, good enough for light work, Bur-rage said. He helped the boys put their wagon together again. Ma wanted to pay him. He shook his head and drove away, with his seven girls all yelling good byes to Missouri and Cree and Ma.

"I guess old Coupland was right about the Topknot," Hugh said. "Let's buy us a few hundred cows and stay right here."

Ma looked out on the Breakwagon Hills. "I think that must be the thing to do."

Long afterward Dirk realized what cour-age and flexibility were necessary for her to make that statement. Now he asked: "How can we buy cows?"

"We can't," Ma said. "We have about enough money to buy food through the winter, if there are any supply wagons coming this way."

"There must be," Talbot said. "Old Burrage said he was going to set up his shop at the river place. All them fire-headed girls got to have something to eat."

"That Rachel was a kind of pretty one," Hugh mused.

Missouri snorted. "Huh! She didn't say the same about you, Hugh Adams Davis Breslin!"

When Dirk realized they were stuck with staying where they were or trying to go back, with a wheel that would not last, he was scared once more. Farming here would be almost impossible. They lacked money to buy cows. All that night he could not sleep. The plateau was hot. The leaves hung silently on the cottonwoods. Dirk heard his mother and the girls stirring restlessly in the wagon. Over and over he thought of the slices of apples his grandfather used to cut for him when they walked together in the orchards. It was torture. Most likely there never would be fruit out here. Or anything else. Just land and no end to it. Dirk was hungry to the point of sickness for just one bite of apple, but he knew it was really not the fruit he craved — he was sick for everything safe and familiar, now lost, far away. Hot and tense he lay on his blanket, staring at the dark sky.

It was odd, he thought, that Hugh had talked so little of Pa from the time the wagon floated across the river. Hugh was not one to forget. Thoughts of Pa came out of the silent night to Dirk. He blinked away tears.

They started a cabin the next day. It was to be a temporary shelter. The green cottonwoods were heavy, and the dry dead ones were like long corkscrews and bitterly hard to cut. Dirk tried to file the axe as he had seen Pa file it, and then it was duller than ever.

"Here, Talbot, you try it."

Talbot did the job, and then the axe was truly sharp. "In a rough country," Talbot said, staring a moment into nowhere, "you get rough yourself to lick it." Pa had said that, away back there where they first saw the hills.

They built a cabin of crooked logs, the corners out of plumb. They daubed it with mud from the marshy ground, and the mud dried and fell out. Hugh killed a deer in the timber farther west, the first large animal he had ever killed. He brought it in on Mitch, leading the horse, half running in his excitement. Talbot was at once interested in the hide and hair. Before long he was chopping hair from the skin with his knife. He mixed the hair with mud and then he had a daubing material that did not fall apart easily even when dry.

"Who told you about that?" Hugh asked.

Talbot shook his head. "Nobody. I never saw a deer before. The idea just come to me, that's all."

Two more wagons of discouraged settlers came by on their way back to the river. They had been too late in the Topknot country; all the land left there was on rocky slopes.

A few days later Judge Coupland rode his Kentucky horse up to the Breslins' cabin. Since they had seen him the last time, he had started to grow a beard — to build up the narrowness of his chin, Missouri said afterward — and he was wearing a wide-brimmed hat.

"I'm glad to see you've decided to settle here, Missus Breslin," Coupland said.

"We didn't decide," Missouri said. "We busted down and had to light."

Coupland laughed. He inspected the outside walls of the cabin and pronounced the structure a good job. When he saw the deer hair in the daubing, he frowned and asked: "Now there's an idea! Yours, Dirk?"

"Him." Dirk pointed at Talbot, who got red in the face and looked at the ground.

"Why, he's three years younger than you, Dirk," Coupland said.

"Yes, but Talbot thinks of things," Missouri said. "Dirk just swallows hard and scowls and gives orders to everybody like he knew what he was doing."

Dirk grinned weakly. "You, Misery," he said, but he knew his sister was right.

Coupland stayed for dinner. He said there was a sort of town beginning to form at the river crossing. "Oh, nothing yet, just the idea, but there will be a town there, I'm sure. I've taken up a town site."

The saloon was still going and another man had started a store in a tent. Judge Coupland spoke of streets and buildings, of a flour mill, a bridge, and other things as if they were already in existence. One thing was sure, Dirk thought — the new land didn't scare Coupland a darned bit. Of course, he was a grown man, and he probably had a lot of money and knew just what he was going to do.

"Hang onto this place, Missus Breslin," Coupland said. "You have rights as a soldier's widow . . . file on this land. I'll help you all I can. Have Dirk bring you to the river as soon as possible so I can get the papers started on their way."

Ma studied the judge. He wasn't much for looks, what with his beard just starting to sprout raggedly on his chin, but there was a sincere expression about him. After a while Ma said: "I'll start back with you today, Mister Coupland."

Missouri was all excited at once. "You mean we'll make our farm here, Ma?"

"I don't know what we'll have," Ma said. She looked around at her family quickly. Dirk could see she was worried. "I'll take the girls with me," she said. "Cree can ride behind me. Missouri can ride Mitch."

The judge watched Dirk and Hugh saddle the horses. "Maybe you boys are too young to know it, but you have a wonderful mother. Take care of her. Help her hold this land. In time you may be able to control the whole south half of the Breakwagon Hills."

Hugh grinned. "Maybe the north half, too." He didn't even know there was a north half.

Coupland pushed his lips out. "Well, I hear that four or five wagons of disappointed folks from the Topknot lit up north of here. You'll have enough to hold this part."

Ma and the girls rode away with Coupland. For once, Lafayette didn't cry. He had accepted the cabin as home.

"We'd better do some exploring," Hugh said to Dirk, "if we're going to own all this country."

III

They rode bareback on Vick and Ten, fat and strong once more from the rich grass of the plateau. Five miles west, from the top of one of the higher hills, they saw only more hills that gathered in little swirls that rose and twisted crazily like the waves of great currents smashing against each other. To the south it was the same, farther than they could see. Groves of cottonwoods stood green and tall to mark a hundred springs. All the land was covered with tall grass. It waved at them from the summits of the hills; it was belly deep on the horses in the troughs between the hills.

Hugh was awed. "I didn't know this was such a big country." On the return trip, when the sun was low, he said with sudden seriousness: "When we going to get that pistol we talked about?"

"We got one already."

"You said we'd get another, Dirk."

"What for do we need it now?"

"Someday we got to go find the man that killed Pa. A man with scorpion eyes and a nice white shirt and big long fingers."

Hugh spoke so coldly and surely that Dirk was shocked. "He's gone away, Hugh. No telling where."

"He won't go too far for me. When are we going to get another pistol, Dirk?"

Dirk thought he should have known better than to make a promise to Hugh, and then try to forget it. He had meant the promise when he made it, but now the memory of Pa was not quite so powerful. Still, he had made the promise. He said: "When we can, we'll get it. There ain't no place around here that sells things like that." And they had no money.

"All right." Hugh showed that he had expected more.

Squire and Tommy Bascomb were sitting on the woodpile when Dirk and Hugh got back to the cabin. Lafayette was on the doorstep. There was a bruise on his cheek, and Dirk saw at once that he had been crying.

"Where's Talbot?" Dirk asked.

"In the house." Lafayette glared at the

Bascombs.

"You hit him, huh?" Dirk said. "You picked on him and Talbot. Now me and Hugh are here."

The Bascombs rose. Squire kept his hand on a short piece of wood. "We didn't come down here for no fight. Pa got hurt, and Ma said to. . . ."

"You hit Lafayette, didn't you?" Hugh accused.

"No, he didn't!" Lafayette cried. "I hit him first. He pushed me over a log, and my face. . . ."

"Picking on a little kid like that." Hugh snatched a piece of wood from the pile and advanced on Squire.

"Nobody got hurt!" Lafayette said. "Talbot was showing me how he would build a bridge like old Coupland said across the river, and Squire stepped on one end of it and busted it, and. . . ."

"Never mind," Dirk said. He picked up another club when he saw Tommy take one.

"Now, look here," Squire said. "We're sorry about the little bridge. I didn't mean to bust it. Pa got hurt, and Ma sent us down here to see if your ma could come. We didn't want to start no fight."

"That's a big lie about your pa, I bet," Hugh said. "Drop that club if you don't

46

want to start no fight."

Squire tossed the firewood back on the pile, and then Tommy did likewise. Hugh threw his club away. "That's better," he said. He hit Squire in the stomach. Dirk rushed in and smothered Tommy just as he reached down to retrieve his club.

Tommy wasn't much of a problem. Sitting on him, Dirk had time to look around at Hugh and Squire. Hugh wasn't having any luck this second time. He just kept boring in and taking a beating. When he tried to butt Squire in the belly, Squire leaped back and Hugh went sprawling.

Talbot came out. Quite calmly he watched a moment when the fight resumed, and then he picked up a piece of wood, hefted it, reversed his grip, and rapped Squire on the head. Squire went down like a pole-axed beef. Still boring in, Hugh fell over him.

"That wasn't fair!" Dirk carried. "Hugh was. . . ."

"You aimed to hurt him, didn't you, Hugh?" Talbot tossed his club away.

"Sure I did! I would have licked him, too, but. . . ."

"Now he's licked. That's the idea of fighting, ain't it?" Talbot was surprised at the reaction to his method of reaching a goal so readily and easily. He went inside. Later,

47

when Dirk went in, Talbot was reading one of Pa's books that told how steam locomotives were made.

Squire got up and staggered around, holding his head.

Dirk felt sorry for him. "You want some water?"

"I want nothing you got. Come on, Tommy." The Bascombs climbed on their horses. "This was a fine thing, Dirk Breslin. We come down here for help when Pa was hurt, maybe dying, and this is what we got."

It was Talbot who had cracked Squire on the head, but Squire talked like it was Dirk. That's what happened when you started being the boss . . . you got all the blame.

The Bascombs rode away. "Maybe their pa *was* hurt," Hugh said. "I kind of like old Bolivar."

"I tried to tell you, me and Talbot wasn't mad at them!" Lafayette shrilled. "Their pa got hurt when a horse fell on him when he was dragging logs for a cabin. We didn't remember when Ma said she was coming back, so they were waiting to ask you and Dirk."

Ma came back from the river place — it was being called Coupland's Crossing by some — two days later. She rode at once north to find the Bascombs' camp, taking Dirk with her.

The cabin was much like the one the Breslins had built, except there were higher hills around and a small spring-fed stream beside it. The Bascombs were burying Bolivar when Ma and Dirk reached there.

Mrs. Bascomb was right glad to see Dirk and Ma. She cried a lot, and Dirk could see she wasn't just carrying on. There never was any mention of the fight between the boys. Before Dirk and Ma left to go home the next day, Dirk was quite sure the Bascomb boys had not said a word at home about the fight. He was real sorry for them, and he tried to say something nice to Squire and Tommy. Tommy was willing to hear, but Squire took him by the arm and led him away from Dirk.

"Somebody down your way may get hurt some time," Squire said. He was almost bawling.

The racket borne in by the hot summer wind was something to scare a person. It came swelling out of the hills southwest of the Breslin place. "Them are cattle!" Hugh cried. He was hopping around with excitement, and then ran to saddle Mitch. Almost immediately he came running back.

"Suppose it's somebody settling on our land with cattle!" he yelled. "You get Pa's pistol, Dirk. I'll get my rifle."

"You get nothing of the sort," Ma said. "That isn't our land down there. You can ride down and see what it is, but that's all."

The land was covered with them, great, high-shouldered brutes with horns as wide as a man's reach. They were thicker than sheep in Grandfather Sterns's east pasture at lambing time. Here and there a rider sat, all slouched and careless, on the hills that overlooked the herd.

Dirk and Hugh worked closer to the smoke they saw. Brindle monsters with wild eyes and clashing horns made way for them readily. Hugh whooped. He kicked at the high backs with bare feet, having a time.

Five men were sitting on bedrolls near a wagon, eating from tin plates. They were all burned dark by the sun, tall men with cold eyes. Although each face was different, there was a mark of similarity about them all. The sixth man, much older than the rest, walked with a limp. But like the rest, he wore a pistol under the dirtiest flour-sack apron Dirk had ever seen.

"Hi, there, buttons," one fellow said. His hat was black, covered with dust and the band was frayed. His eyes were the cold color of Hugh's eyes when he was fighting, but they were bedded in friendly crinkles and the man's voice was soft, with a long drawl to it. "Light down and get your grub."

"You fellows figure to settle here?" Dirk swallowed hard.

The blue-eyed man said: "Just for a few days, son. Your land?"

Dirk nodded. They were all staring at his bare feet. Hugh was ready to eat but he was uncertain about the preliminaries.

"Plate there in the wreck pan, kid," one of the fellows said.

Hugh looked all around him. "There!" the cook said sourly, pointing at a dishpan with plates on edge in water. "There ain't nothing wrong with 'em. Chaco and the day guard just et off them plates, that's all. Slosh one around and give it a swipe on your sleeve."

"He ain't got much sleeve left, Cookie," one of the cowpunchers said.

Dirk and Hugh sloshed and swiped. There was pan bread and beans, poured over with molasses, and coffee to float a wedge.

The blue-eyed man's name was Rusty. He was burned so dark Dirk couldn't see any reason for the name until the fellow tipped his hat back and revealed a thatch of dark red hair. The others were Luke, Brazos,

Hull, and Johnny. They called the cook about four different names, never the same one twice. After a while Rusty told the crew to circle around the herd and see that no cattle were straying.

"I get seasick here," Brazos said. "Ain't there no level ground anywhere in this country?"

"Over by our place," Hugh said. "We got a nice flat stretch over there."

"I'll come over," Brazos said. "Just so I can lay down straight. Every night it's the same. I sleep with my feet up on one hill, my back up another, and my rear end in the bottom of a gully. I'm gradually taking the shape of a horseshoe."

"You'll make it," Rusty said. "Wait till we start north again. If we run into what we've heard about, you'll wish you had a gully to jump into."

Hugh kept looking at the pistol on Rusty's hip. "What's one of them worth?"

"Your life," Rusty said, "when you need to use it."

"I mean money."

"What for do you need a pistol, button?"

"I got to kill a man someday," Hugh said.

"Yeah?"

"He's a gambler. He killed our father."

Rusty accepted it just as Hugh gave it.

Dirk was startled. He could see that Hugh and Rusty seemed to understand each other very well.

"Take a pistol like this," Rusty said, "it's worth about seven steers." He looked north. "Might be worth the whole herd."

"What's up there?" Hugh asked.

"Some people. This'll be the second Texas herd that's tried to get through."

"I ain't got seven steers," Hugh said. "But I need a gun like that, Rusty."

The words were downright begging, Dirk thought, but they didn't seem to strike Rusty that way. He kept looking at Hugh, and there was something that passed between him and Dirk's brother that left Dirk standing apart, removed from their tight circle of understanding.

"Who are the men folks in your outfit?" Rusty asked.

"Us," Hugh said. "We own all this land." He swept his arm around carelessly. "When we get some cows, we'll have the biggest ranch there ever was."

Rusty smiled thinly. "You ever see a big ranch in big country, bub?"

"No," Dirk said. "This will be big enough for us."

Rusty looked from one of them to the other. The oldness and the hardness of his face had not been so obvious until this moment when, by contrast, a half-musing boyish smile changed his features. He looked then not much older that the two who faced him. "I used to think I'd have a ranch someday myself." He went to his horse and swung up. The toughness was on him again. "Ride over another time," he said. "We'll be here a few more days."

His leggy dun went up a steep hill with a powerful surge. Hugh looked sadly at old Put and Mitch.

The cook was washing dishes. He eyed them with disfavor. "You won't ever have no ranch by standing around," he said.

They thanked him for the food and rode away.

"What was the idea of begging for a pistol?"

"It wasn't begging. I just told him I needed one. He knew it, too."

Rusty had understood, Dirk admitted, but he himself could not understand and knew he would never understand the thing that had passed between Hugh and the Texan. They were alike in one manner.

Twice more the boys rode to the camp, staying longer each time. On their way home the second time, Hugh said: "Those fellows are going to move tomorrow."

"They didn't say so."

"Couldn't you tell? They didn't talk any and joke with each other like before. There's a gang of whites and Indians north of here where they're going. Rusty said they wiped out the drovers of the first herd that tried to go through. We ought to go along to help, Dirk."

"They wouldn't let us and you know it!"

"We didn't ask. They're our friends, and, besides, we'd get a pistol out of it, maybe two. They all got extra pistols."

"You want a pistol awful bad, don't you?"

"I got to have it," Hugh said simply. "You know why."

It was true that Pa's old pistol wasn't much shakes. Dirk sighed. The country was tough, all right, and Hugh was growing tough along with it. Dirk thought of the peaceful farms back home. Now the thought carried only a contrast, and not a desire to retreat.

"We can't do it, Hugh. Not for a dozen pistols."

"I guess not." Hugh began to whistle.

The bawling of the longhorns was more frenzied than ever at daylight the next morning. Standing in the pearl-gray dawn in front of the Breslin cabin, the Breslin boys listened to the sounds rolling up from the green hills. Hugh and Dirk could read them now. They knew when the bawling began to subside that the herd had been lined out and was moving north.

"I thought maybe Rusty would come by," Hugh said when the herd was almost out of earshot. He did not sound disappointed. Dirk watched him suspiciously, but all that day Hugh gave no sign that the going of the cattle had left any void in him.

He was gone at dawn the next day, and so was Mitch. Dirk restrained an urge to run and throw a saddle on old Put immediately, but there was no use to get his mother and the others upset.

"Well, Hugh went hunting again, I guess," Dirk said at breakfast.

Ma Breslin nodded, but Dirk saw at once that she knew better. The younger ones didn't seem to catch on, but Missouri said: "Hunting, your foot! He run off with that bunch of cowboys and you know it. Ever since they've been here, Hugh has been like a hop toad on hot cinders."

"Missouri," Ma said.

"Well, he . . . ," Missouri subsided.

"He might need help with his deer, Dirk," Ma said. "Maybe you'd better ride after him. I worry sometimes about him hunting all by himself."

Dirk would have leaped away at once, but his mother held him at the table with her glance.

She stood beside him when he saddled old Put. Her fear was then stark. "Why did he do it, Dirk?"

"Rusty and the others are our friends and they're going to have a fight."

"A gunfight . . . ? He won't be sixteen until next month." Ma looked way off into distance. Still fifteen, but he was big enough for twenty, and he could stand before a man like Rusty and talk like a man. He wanted a pistol like the Texan carried, and he was willing to go into a fight to gain it. "Put your shoes on, Dirk," Ma said. "You'd better wear them all the time now. Go by the Bascombs' and ask. . . ."

"I don't need Squire's help."

"In this land everyone needs the help of everyone else foolish enough to come here." Ma wasn't given to talking like that. It rattled Dirk. He fumbled with the cinch. "No," she said an instant later. "It was not foolish to come here. Bring him back, Dirk."

For a while Dirk was afraid he might not be able to follow the trail, but he was never off it. Gradually his confidence in that matter was restored. He didn't know exactly when Hugh had left, but he did know when the herd had moved out of the hills southeast of the Breslin place. He figured two days would be enough for him to catch up.

Before long he learned of the traveling abilities of longhorn cattle. Four nights he camped, and by then he was across the steep buff sandstone escarpment that separated the north and south parts of the Breakwagon Hills, and he was deep into sagebrush country where there were only miles and sky ahead of him — and no dust cloud on the horizon. Off to the left were the mountains, standing purple and gray. Beyond them lay the Topknot. Antelope skimmed across the flats before him. He followed them with Pa's old rifle, clicking his tongue instead of the trigger, wondering where his shots would have gone, wondering, too, whether he could shoot a man if he reached the herd before the trouble started. Maybe there would be no trouble. But he remembered the lean hard faces that last night at the campfire, and the silence of the Texans.

On the sixth day, when he had no food except salt to put on antelope meat, it came to him why he was not gaining as he should have. Old Put was slow, it was true, but for several days, Dirk decided, the herd had been traveling this flat country by night as well as by day, resting only briefly at water holes.

The eighth day came racing over the sage, bursting quickly on all the vast horizons. Dirk had no idea of where he was or how far he had gone. The tracks of the herd were still there before him, and that was all. It was mid-morning when he heard the firing far ahead. There was nothing he could see up there. He was alone in the middle of distance.

Put stopped and threw his head high, listening, and then he lost interest in the sounds. Dirk sat there, scared and lonely, with one hand resting on the hot gray hairs of old Put's shoulder. It sounded to Dirk like one of the battles Pa used to talk about. Dirk went ahead at a trot.

The firing went on and on. It must be a hell of a fight, Dirk thought. He kept swallowing. Pa's rifle was across his knees, loaded and cocked. There came the sounds of bawling longhorns again, and before long cattle were streaming toward him. They broke around old Put and went on, long-legged brutes that ran as if they would reach Texas before nightfall. Then, to the left and right, far ahead, he saw the dust of other racing steers. The herd must have been in a depression, around a brackish water hole such as ones Dirk had passed. Where was Hugh? Dirk tried to make old Put gallop, but he did well to keep him going against the cattle. Put wanted to turn and run with them.

All at once the longhorns were gone. Now the firing was almost done. Ahead of Dirk was dust that veiled everything. He heard the sound of a rifle bullet somewhere off to his left. He ducked. He felt he was too high in the saddle, and so he leaped down and went on, leading old Put into the dust. It began to settle, and then he saw three riders coming toward him at a gallop. One, he was sure, was on Rusty's dun; a little later he recognized Mitch and saw Hugh, hatless, his straw-colored hair flapping wildly.

There where five or six riders chasing the first three. When Dirk saw them, fear clutched his stomach with a twisting grip. He wanted to run, but he was afraid to turn his back to the sound of bullets that whistled overhead once more. Rusty and the others did not fire back. They merely rode.

They came up to Dirk as he stood with the knotted end of the reins in the crook of one elbow, with his rifle lifted above the sage toward the five horsemen. He was aware that Hugh was alive, unharmed, that Rusty's face was full of bitterness and shame, that Brazos was gray and open-mouthed. Dirk lined his rifle on a dark horse scudding close to the sage. It was an antelope, he told himself. The old rifle roared. Rank powder smoke swirled back in Dirk's face. He saw the rider standing in air for an instant and then a great bloom of fresh dust where the horse and man went tumbling.

"Let 'em in close!" Rusty said. "I lost my rifle back there." He was standing beside Dirk with his hot pistol still in his hand.

Brazos had fallen from his horse and was lying on his back, breathing hard. Hugh came running over to Dirk. "Gimme some shells!"

"Won't fit your rifle," Dirk mumbled. He was watching a gray horse now, and was almost ready to fire again.

"They fit my pistol!" Hugh said. He dug into his brother's pocket.

"Let 'em come right in," Rusty said. "All the way."

Dirk didn't want them any closer. He did not want to see clearly a man's face or form when he shot. He knocked the gray horse over.

Dirk dropped three cartridges when he tried to reload. He stooped to find them in the dust, and, when he rose again three horses, two carrying double, were going away from him.

Rusty cursed. "The two on the roan, Dirk!"

Dirk stared at them. They were running away. He lowered the rifle. Rusty grabbed it from him. He shot and the man riding behind the saddle on the roan fell backward over the horse's rump. Before Rusty reloaded, the horses were well out of rifle range.

Rusty handed the rifle back. "I don't generally grab a man's gun thataway." He went over to Brazos and asked quietly: "How bad?"

Brazos rolled his head, smiling. There was blood on his lips. "I won't see Texas this fall, Rusty."

IV

They camped that night where the sage was head high around the slick sides of a water hole. Brazos died in the dark, with Rusty sitting beside him, telling him how Texas would look when they reached there in a few weeks.

The last thing Brazos said was: "Don't let anybody take my boots off, Rusty. They're still on, ain't they?"

"Still on, son. You'll wear 'em back to that little place on the Canadian. You'll. . . ."

Afterwards Rusty sat alone in the dark. "You two get some rest," he said.

Several times during the night Dirk heard Rusty prowling wide circles around the camp. In a bare space where the ground was honeycombed by prairie dogs, they buried Brazos the next day. Rusty gave one of his pistols to Hugh and the other one, with the belt and holster, to Dirk. Dirk thought he knew why he got the best of it: he had blundered up at a critical time and, too scared to run, he had given Rusty and Hugh a chance to stand and fight. Later, he would give the belt and holster to Hugh.

"They didn't get all the herd," Hugh said. "Some of them ran south." He was wearing a pair of cowboy boots now. His old shoes were hanging on his saddle horn.

"They got enough." Rusty was tense and bitter. They never saw him smile again. "It was my blunder, thinking we wouldn't get jumped in the middle of daylight."

They went on up to the water hole. The wagon was gone. The raiders had stripped the bodies of the dead Texans. Someone had hacked off Hull's finger to get a ring. "He gave me these boots, Hull did," Hugh said, bitter then as Rusty who muttered to himself in Spanish while they were burying the cowboys in the gray land.

In the northern Breakwagons they found part of the herd. The Bascomb boys were looking at them from the top of a hill. Squire didn't budge when Hugh ran his horse at him.

"Don't try to steal none of these!" Hugh said.

"Who was?" Squire looked at Hugh's pistol. "They're on our land."

"You're sure claiming plenty of country, Squire."

"So are you Breslins . . . and acting big with them guns stuck in your belt." The Bascombs rode away.

Rusty had not spoken all day. Now he said, watching Squire and Tommy: "You got two things you can do . . . make up with them boys so the northern end of your range will always be protected . . . or run 'em clear out of the country." He talked, Dirk thought, like the Breslins had a ranch already.

They pushed 113 cattle across the escarpment and into the southern part of the Breakwagons. "Culls," Rusty said. "Trail stuff. I'll come up this way next summer and I'll bring you a bull."

"You mean you're leaving the cattle here?"

Dirk said.

Rusty was savage in an instant. "Do you think I'm driving 'em back to Texas?"

"How about the man who owns 'em?"

"I own 'em," Rusty said. "Now they're yours. I guess it wasn't in the cards for me to be nothing but a hand. I crossed the Big Red with a thousand and thirty-three head of mavericks. The farther we went, the tighter my hat got on my head . . . let it be a lesson to you two. You'll have to fight like hell for everything you get, and then twice as hard to hang onto it." He looked north toward the escarpment. "Was I you boys, I'd smoke the pipe with those two we saw the other day. From the looks of that oldest one, they ain't going to do much running."

Rusty had seen Squire Bascomb just once. He had sized Squire about right, Dirk thought.

"Now you got cattle and you got pistols," Rusty said. "You better learn how to handle both." He started the dun south.

"Hey!" Dirk said. "You can stay with us."

Rusty did not look back or hesitate. "Thanks, but this ain't my country." He rode into the southern sun, with the dust gray on his jacket and his black hat low to his eyes.

Dirk unstrapped the pistol belt and gave it

to Hugh. He put his own pistol in his waistband. Pa had worn his gun like that the morning he had walked confidently toward the tent saloon. As soon as possible Dirk would get himself another belt.

Pa had been right, and Rusty had been right. You had to get tough with the country. But Dirk kept remembering the Texans he had helped bury. He doubted that he had the stomach for being tough. He did not even have the desire. But now the Breslins were in the cattle business, and there would be people who would try to profit from the fact. Responsibility came down heavily on Dirk.

Hugh was sighting down his pistol. "What will we call this here outfit, Dirk?"

"The Brazos." B for Breslin — and the name of a man they had scarcely known, but he had fought beside Hugh, and he had smiled when he knew he was dying. The country needed that sort. Dirk had the feeling that he and Hugh had caught hold of something they could not easily release.

By the time they reached home Dirk's confidence was rising again. After all, they had done quite a bit in the last two weeks. They went through the grove of trees, past the spring, and up to the yard feeling happy.

The silence said no one lived here. They

stared at each other, with their color fading.

"Hey!" Hugh cried. "Hey, Ma!"

Talbot came out of the house slowly. He blinked wearily, with his jaw sagging.

"Dirk and Hugh," he muttered.

He leaned against the logs, and then slid down them to the ground and lay there. One moment they had been in the hard clean freedom of the hills, healthy young animals filled with a keen anticipation of homecoming. Now they stood where, it seemed, death had already struck. Not the violent shock of death they had seen around the water hole, that had come hard and swiftly, but the insidious, baffling creep of sickness.

Ma was in one bed with Missouri and Cree, and Lafayette was in his bed. Their faces were aglow with fever. Missouri was muttering to herself. A panicky terror that he hadn't felt from the song of bullets overhead gushed up to leave a coppery tang in Dirk's mouth.

"What'll we do, Dirk?" The smudge of campfires and the dust of riding lay on Hugh's face, and underneath he was white and stricken and young. "What'll we do, Dirk! What's the matter with them?"

"I don't know." Dirk stood several moments in the middle of the room, every instinct of his healthy body rejecting sickness. "Measles, maybe," he said.

"We all had measles!" Hugh picked up Talbot and carried him to the bed beside Lafayette. "He ain't hot at all, Dirk."

Dirk moved at last. He put his palm on Talbot's forehead. There was no fever. It came to him that Talbot was worn out from worrying and trying to take care of everyone else. His spirit had carried him until he saw relief, and then he had collapsed.

"Drink . . . Ma . . . ," Missouri muttered.

"Go get Missus Bascomb, Hugh," Dirk said. He wanted to go himself, to run away — therefore he stayed. He had done things like that ever since Pa's death.

He heard Mitch go into a run. He sponged the faces on the beds with cool water. He gave them water when they called for it, and, once during the endless day and the day that followed, Missouri looked at him with recognition and spoke his name. Then she slipped away into the red mists once more. Talbot was helping then. All he knew was that everyone had taken sick just a few days after Hugh and Dirk rode north.

Mrs. Bascomb came with Callie and Hugh that night. She walked into the room with a quickness surprising for her size. "Well," she said, "the whole danged layout, nearly,

68

just like Hugh said." There was something reassuring in her manner.

"What is it they got?" Dirk asked.

"I'd say slow fever. That's as good a guess as any."

"Will they all die?"

"The Lord will have that say, but Callie and me will try to influence Him a little. Now them that can walk, clear out and give us a chance."

Hugh and Dirk and Talbot sat close together on the woodpile. From the cabin Mrs. Bascomb's voice boomed out cheerfully, giving orders to Callie, giving orders to the sick Breslins just as if they could hear and understand.

Once she came to the doorway and looked out. "You boys get to bed," she said. "And do some praying before you go to sleep, mind me."

The Breslin boys climbed into the wagon. "You two do what she said," Dirk ordered fiercely.

"All right," Talbot said, "but tomorrow I'm going to clean that spring out. I been thinking everybody that camped here on the way to the Topknot might have thrown something dirty into it."

Dirk prayed silently that his mother and all the rest would get well. He promised to give half the cattle to the Bascombs, whether his folks got well or not. When that was done, he reached over and touched Hugh, who was still wearing his pistol belt and pistol.

"Did you pray, Hugh?"

Hugh was asleep.

The Breslins lived. They were weak for a long time, and Ma complained that she could scarcely walk ten feet without wanting to sit down. Mrs. Bascomb stayed ten days the first time, and she came back several times more during the late summer. Callie and Hugh were giggling at each other before it was over.

By then what Hugh and Dirk had done up north with Rusty was lost under the pressure of other events; they told only that Rusty had given them the cattle after his bunch had some bad trouble.

On a sharp fall day Dirk rode out with Hugh and Talbot to look at the cattle. The longhorns had found the grass of the Breakwagon Hills to their liking. Talbot was wearing Pa's old pistol now. They stopped for target practice. Talbot was the slowest of the three, but he was the best shot. He used two hands and aimed carefully.

"We got to have a lot of shells," Dirk said.

"We'll take a steer or two to the river place and see what we can do." And then he told them what he had promised to do with half the cattle.

"Oh, hell!" Hugh said. "Tommy and Squire didn't help Rusty's bunch any."

"Missus Bascomb helped us," Dirk said. "We'll give half the cattle to her, not the boys."

"The same thing," Hugh grumbled. "But since you made the promise. . . . If I hadn't fallen asleep that night, I would have promised only one third." He thought a while, then he laughed.

They had one devil of a time cutting out half the herd. The longhorns seemed to skim the ridges and soar up the steep hills. Dirk had carried the thought of picking out the poorest of the bunch, since his promise involved numbers only, but before it was over he settled on anything they could separate from the herd. They drove fifty-four head north. That was a little short of half but Dirk figured the Lord must have seen how hard longhorns were to handle. They pushed them as close as they could to the Bascomb place, and then the boys rode on in.

Callie and Hugh began to moon at each other immediately. Tommy and Talbot got

71

friendly too, but Dirk and Squire just looked at each other. "We brought you half our herd, Missus Bascomb," Dirk said. "Almost half. There was some we couldn't catch."

"Why are you doing this?"

The question and the steady inquiry of Mrs. Bascomb's eyes disconcerted Dirk. He said: "You helped us . . . and, besides, I guess you need 'em." There was also a feeling of guilt from the time Squire and Tommy had ridden down for help when their father was dying.

Mrs. Bascomb glanced toward the hill where Bolivar was buried. She seemed to understand everything in Dirk's mind. "Well, for heaven's sake, come in and eat! Callie, stop making sheep's eyes at that ugly no-account Hugh and set the table!" There were tears in Mrs. Bascomb's eyes.

Squire said: "We don't need their cattle, Ma." He took a step toward Dirk. "We don't need nothing from you, Dirk Breslin."

"Squire!" Ma Bascomb said. "That's no way. . . ."

"Uhn-huh." Squire shook his head. "Take your cows back."

It came to Dirk that Mrs. Bascomb was no longer the complete boss here, just as Ma Breslin was no longer the leader in the Breslin home. Dirk saw in Squire some of

72

the same qualities he possessed, only stronger and more clearly defined. They both had started to grow up fast under the pressure of the country and loss of fathers.

"I want you to have the cattle, Squire."

Squire shook his head.

"Let's go, Hugh," Dirk said.

"Take your cattle with you!"

Hugh and Dirk rode away, leaving the Bascombs wrangling. They were all upbraiding Squire.

Hugh grinned about it. "He'll have to take 'em. He can't hold out against all that racket."

That was probably true, Dirk thought, but Squire wouldn't be pleased, and he would blame Hugh and Dirk for putting him in a spot where he would have to back down.

The Breslins drove three cows to the river place. They started with four, but one turned back and they couldn't head it. "We got to have some horses," Hugh grumbled. "Ours were never nothing but wagon horses to begin with."

"First we got to have plenty of shells," Dirk said. He was thinking of the raiders who had taken the Texas herd. If the Brazos ranch — the name wasn't sticking too well in his mind yet — and the Bascomb place

73

began to prosper a little, they would inevitably draw attention from the shadowy men up north.

The river was down now. There was a ferry cable across it and a boat. It took Talbot just a minute to figure out how the current could be used to pull the boat both ways.

"Houses over there now," Hugh said.

They pushed the three cows into the stream. There were only two deep places where all the animals were forced to swim. The Breslins felt important when they emerged on the other side, with men looking at them from every doorway. Now there were two saloons, a wooden store building, and a real estate office.

Judge Coupland came from the real estate office. "I've missed you boys. How's your ma? Where have you been all summer?"

"Most of the folks was sick," Hugh said. "We thought you might be out, but. . . ."

"I was gone all summer," Coupland said. "Just got back two days ago from trying to raise money and settlers back East. I got some of the last, but the first is sort of scarce. Your cattle?"

"We come by them fair and honest," Dirk said.

Coupland nodded toward the store. "Ben

Carmody can use them. How much do you want?"

The Breslins looked at each other.

"Eight dollars a head is not bad," Coupland said. "You'll have to take half of it in trade, I imagine."

Dirk and Talbot went into the store with Coupland. There was very little on shelves but considerable in boxes on the floor. Parts of the carcasses of two steers were hanging near a butcher block at the back of the room. Carmody was a thin man with a wide spade beard and sad brown eyes.

"You need some more meat, Ben," Coupland said.

Carmody shook his head, pointing at the steers.

"Sell it, sell it!" Coupland said. "What are you keeping it here for?"

"I could sell plenty of everything," Carmody said sadly, "all on credit."

"That's the ticket, Ben! Everything out here is credit. You lose a lot, of course, but in the end you make a town. We got three prime steers outside. . . ."

"Cows," Dirk said.

"Three prime pieces of meat," Coupland said. "Ten dollars a head. Put up a few signs. When folks want credit, let 'em have it."

75

"That's what broke me back home," Carmody said.

"If you go bust, we all do," Coupland said. "Then we'll go on and try again. Ten dollars a head, then?"

"You trample a man under, Judge," Carmody said. "Seven."

"Prime stock, Ben. Make it nine dollars a head."

"Eight. All in trade."

"Half in trade," Dirk said.

It was settled.

Outside, Coupland said: "Tell your ma I'll be out in a few days." He gathered up three men from the crowd that had grown around the cows, and took them up the street toward his office. Two of them didn't seem to want to go badly, but Coupland took them along, talking a steady stream about the advantages of buying lots and settling in Coupland's Crossing.

Dirk divided the boxes of ammunition he had taken in part trade for the cows. They drove the animals to a corral behind the store.

"Somebody sold four steers here two days ago," Hugh said. "They had Rusty's trail brand on 'em. The fellows, two of 'em, are down the street in the River Saloon right now, a man said."

"Let them stay there," Dirk said.

"They're sure to be two of the bunch that ruined us at the water hole," Hugh said. "They'll come down our way sooner or later, won't they?"

Dirk had thought the same thing himself. "What do you want to do about them? Anyway, Rusty said he was coming back next spring . . . and he won't be alone."

"He ain't here now," Hugh said. "They are."

Talbot was white. He said calmly: "Let Hugh look at them. If they're the ones he's talking about, the best thing to do is walk in and shoot them."

Dirk understood that it was a mechanical principle with Talbot, just a matter of going from one point to another in the simplest manner, but the coldness of the logic frightened him.

"Would you do that, Talbot?"

"If we had to, I would . . . talking about something is no good."

"Well?" Hugh said.

"We'll go down and look at them."

Hugh's eyes had turned pale. He was looking past Dirk. Two men were walking toward the corral, two whiskery men in ragged clothes. They were both about the same size, stocky men, dark-eyed and loose-lipped.

"That's them," Hugh breathed. "I remember those two. They killed Hull."

The pair came up to the corral. They looked at the trail brand on the cows and they looked at the Breslin boys and laughed.

One of them said: "Looks like we missed a few, Arn."

"Some of the bunch that ran south," Arn said. "Where'd you kids get them cows?"

Hugh said: "They're ours, mister."

"Stealing cattle is a hanging offense, son," Arn said. "How about that, Aaron?"

"Yeah," Aaron said, grinning. "It's" — suddenly he reached out and lifted Hugh's hat — "that stack of tow hair there, Arn . . . remember? There were three that rode south. Remember?"

Arn said softly: "Uhn-huh, now I do."

How foolish he and his brothers had been talking. Dirk saw it all now — these two men could kill the three of them before the Breslins knew what was going on. Hugh had doubled up his fists, but now he realized that and was getting geared to reach for his pistol.

Dirk stepped between him and the two men. "Those are our cows," Dirk said.

Arn grinned. "No bill of sale, I'll bet. We'll

78

let it go this time, but if you boys got any more cattle, we'll have to ride down and see about it one of these days. We can't have cattle stealing around here."

"No," Aaron said. "That wouldn't do at all."

The two men were laughing when the Breslins walked away. Dirk was in a cold rage because lies and injustice always revolted him. Hugh was stony-faced and silent because he thought he had failed. Only Talbot saw it clearly enough to speak of it.

"It's lucky we didn't get any ideas about being pistol fighters," he said.

It occurred to Dirk to tell Judge Coupland of the matter, but what could Coupland do? There was no law here, and it might be a long time before there ever was.

The Breslins tied their gunnysacks of supplies on their saddles and went across the river. On the way home they practiced with their pistols.

Missouri told them immediately that three families of farmers, baked out of the Topknot country after a hard summer, had settled near the Big Springs south of the Breslin place.

"That's not really our land," Ma said. "I don't know what we can do about it."

"We can run 'em off!" Dirk said.

79

Talbot asked: "Because we got run off in town?"

"Shut up, Talbot." Dirk thought about it. It was true enough that he was smarting because he had been forced to turn away from a situation. But there was also the fact that settlers in the Breakwagons would start tearing up the grass and building fences. Let them once get started, no matter how hard the soil was to plow, and they would creep all around the Breslins, ruining the land for cattle.

"The first thing in the morning," Dirk said, "we'll have to go run those people out."

Ma sighed. She saw the same things Dirk saw. "Talk to them," she said. "Show them that the land will never be good for farming."

V

They had hitched six horses to a plow, with a man on each handle. Even then it was killing work against the tough grass roots. All three families were working together on it, Dirk guessed, because there were enough kids and women in the Big Springs grove for at least three families.

One of the farmers reminded Dirk of Pa. The other two were little men, hard-handed, with furrowed faces. They stopped their work and greeted the Breslins civilly.

Dirk slouched in the saddle. Being on a horse gave him an advantage, he thought. Already it was setting him apart in his own mind from men who walked.

"This ain't much of a country for farming," he said.

One of the little men wiped sweat and grinned. "Give us time, bud. We're only scratching now, but we'll have fifty acres busted come spring. Once that sod is turned up so the weather and sun can start the roots to rotting, we'll have the grass licked."

"Not much water though," Dirk said.

"The springs'll do."

The man who looked like Pa caught on first. His eyes narrowed, but he asked good naturedly: "What's on your mind?"

"You'll have to move," Hugh said. "This is our land."

"You got filing right on it?"

Dirk shook his head.

"Then nobody moves."

"We got cattle here," Dirk said. "The land is ours by right of use." He had heard Rusty use the expression.

"There ain't no such thing," one of the men said. "Come on, boys, let's get back to our work."

The change in the nature of the conversation had carried to the grove, and now the women and some of the older kids were coming out.

"Don't start the teams," Hugh said. His pistol was out.

The tall man laughed. "Well, by Ned, boys! Three snub-nosed brats on plow horses themselves. . . ." He spoke to the teams.

Hugh fired into the ground three times under the bellies of the lead team. The horses snorted and reared, then lunged ahead. One man still clinging to the handle on his side of the plow was thrown over it as the point went deep and jammed into the grass roots.

The Breslins stood by with drawn pistols and watched the three families load their gear and drive away toward the river, and then they rode behind them half the day. Dirk saw everything that he had seen in his own family, and it sickened him. But Pa would not have run so easily.

This could have happened to the Breslins, but they had been pure lucky. Dirk did not like it at all; he had to keep telling himself that it had been necessary. Neither Hugh nor Talbot took any pride in the victory, and all three of them could remember that they had walked away from two men at the corral behind Ben Carmody's store.

There was one thing Dirk knew for sure — they were one step closer to holding on to the Breakwagons. They would have to see Coupland about getting some legal claim to the land. That business of possession by right of use did not seem very strong.

On the way home the Breslins practiced with their pistols some more. Talbot was still the best shot, and he still held Pa's gun in both hands when he aimed. The boys did not talk about the farmers they had scared away.

When they got home, Ma looked at them and said in a quick, scared voice: "What happened?"

"They left," Dirk said. "Nobody got hurt, except a plow was busted and some harness torn up."

"Do we have to do these things?"

"If we're going to keep these hills, we do."

"If someone is killed, then will the whole land be worth it?"

"I don't know," Dirk said. "Do we want to stay here or not?" That, he realized after he had spoken, was where the truth lay.

"A land of violence," Ma said. She went inside.

The next morning the Breslins took a turn

around the west side of their land to see about the cattle. They took Lafayette along on Ten, with only a rope halter as a rig. Lafayette, it seemed to Dirk, had more natural ease on a horse than any of them. Dirty brindle cattle tossed their horns at the four riders, but the longhorns were getting used to the range now and were not as wild as they had been. Yet, they were wild enough.

"They ought to be branded," Hugh said.

"How do we do that?"

"Rusty told me. We'll have Josh Burrage make us a stamp iron the next time we go to Coupland's Crossing. Then you rope a critter and dump him and burn the brand on him."

"How do you dump him?" Lafayette wanted to know.

"I saw Rusty do it," Hugh said.

"I saw Brazos take one by the tail one day and flip him end-over-katip, too," Dirk said. "But I don't think one of us could do that, even if our horses could get close enough."

"That little mare of Squire's that was so skinny on the wagon . . . she's pretty fast," Talbot said. "Maybe we'd better work with the Bascombs."

"We should have warned them about those two fellows, anyway," Dirk said.

"We better go do that right away."

■ ■ ■ ■

Ma Bascomb said Squire and Tommy had gone to the river with six head to trade for supplies and pistols.

"Half the stuff you given is gone now," she said. "Tommy seen six, seven men round them up, bold as you please, and take 'em away north just yesterday."

"Didn't he do nothing?" Hugh asked.

"What could he do . . . him without a gun of no kind?"

"He couldn't do a thing," Dirk said. "What did we do in town, Hugh, when there were only two men and we had pistols?"

"Well, we'll do something the next time," Hugh said. He stared after Callie when she went toward the spring with a bucket. "You figure out something, Dirk, and then we'll do it."

"There was a full bucket of water in there a minute ago," Ma Bascomb said. "I'll swear that Callie girl throwed it out the window." She shook her head. "Come in for some tea, Dirk and Talbot. We'll have to talk about things."

The tea, Dirk guessed, must be better for a man than the bitter coffee he had drunk around the Texans' fire. He said: "We've got to stand together. If Squire will have it, we'd best drive your cows south of the big hill to our land. They'll be a little harder to get at there. Then we'd better brand 'em. After that. . . ." He didn't know what came after that.

"We can start your herd down today," Talbot said. "If Squire will have it."

"I'm still the oldest one in this family," Ma Bascomb said, "but I will allow that Squire ain't no brat to be slapped any more. Take them cows, like you say."

On the way down with the cattle, Hugh tried to tail over a big blue steer with white spots. He fell off his horse and was knocked cold. The herd scattered while his brothers stood around him. It took two and a half days to move the cattle. The Breslins lived on deer meat roasted over fires on sticks, without salt.

"You got to get tough with the country, I guess," Hugh said, "but I'm sure hungry."

On the last day of the drive he tried tailing another steer. He didn't flip it, but he made it bawl and he did not fall off his horse.

"There's a way to do that," Talbot said. "I been figuring it out, but I'm not about to try the idea."

Judge Coupland was at the cabin when

the boys returned. He had heard about their driving off the settlers.

"The right of use," he said, "is recognized more or less in some localities. It depends on how well you make it stick. The best thing, however, is for each of you boys to file on land. There seems to be a certain elasticity about fulfilling all the requirements. Strictly speaking . . . file on the land. I'll help with the details."

The way the judge was looking at Ma, with his mind only half on his words, Dirk thought he knew now why Coupland had been so helpful. It was a jolt to think of things that way, considering that Pa had been gone only a few months. But out here things seemed to move a little faster than back home.

When Squire and Tommy came down to see about their cattle, they both were wearing pistols. Squire was not quite as set against Dirk as he had been before. And Missouri — it became evident to Dirk that she thought Squire was all right.

Dirk told the Bascombs what Judge Coupland had said about filing homesteads, and so both groups went to town together to get that job started. Coupland was quite helpful in filling out the papers for them. He said he would take them to the Land Office later, and although, he added, it was generally necessary for the persons filing to appear in the flesh, he said he had an understanding with the agent.

He leaned back in his chair. "Good farming land north of here a few miles," he said. "All it needs is a big canal from the river. Cattle country west, with maybe some small prosperity on the Topknot. Why, we'll have a great town here in good time. I've set aside a lot for each one of you boys. Someday you can pay me for them."

The judge believed in dealing the way he had advised Ben Carmody to do business, Dirk thought.

"One more thing," Coupland said. He opened a drawer and laid a pistol on his desk. "When you need a little help out your way . . . and you're going to, I fear . . . let me know."

He was mild, and he was also tough enough, Dirk decided.

The Breslins and the Bascombs were a bruised and sorry lot before they put their stamp irons on the last of their cattle. They learned that a steer or a cow has no love for a man on foot, that a branding iron should not be allowed to burn clean through the hide or used so lightly that it leaves only a hair brand, that a quick leap to the saddle and a rope across a steer's back must have saved many a man before them.

They learned a lot. They put the mark of their possession on longhorns. BR for the Breslins, Circle B for the Bascombs.

When the job was done, they took two days rest to let their burns and bruises heal. It was during that two days that eight men rode south across the escarpment and stole twenty head, driving them north without undue haste. In fact, the thieves had camped the first night within a day's easy ride of the Breslin cabin.

Squire said bleakly: "They figure widows and a bunch of kids are easy pickings. What are we going to do?"

"We could get Judge Coupland," Dirk said, but he had already rejected the idea. You had to stand up to the country and the men in it, or else you didn't belong in the country, or had no right to run squatters off the land and stamp a mark on cattle.

"Where do they take the cattle they steal?" Tommy asked. He was fingering his pistol.

"To the mining country way up north, I guess," Dirk said.

"How far is that?" Squire asked.

"It must be a long trip." Dirk thought of the days he had traveled the sage land, with only the sky and distance for company.

"They don't take 'em all up north," Talbot said. "That Arn and Aaron sold some of them in town."

That was it. "If they do it again, there'll be a brand on every one," Dirk said. "Let's go to town."

When they reached the cottonwood cabin, Callie had just come down from the Bascomb place to say that a farmer was settling on the meadow east of the Bascombs'.

"We'll see about that later," Squire said.

Ma Breslin wanted to know what the boys intended to do if they found some of their cattle sold in town.

"Then we'll find the men," Hugh said.

They rode through the clear autumn air, five boys who were ranchers more or less by accident. At the willows along the river the water was low and green. From their side of the river they saw five critters in Carmody's corral.

Dirk swallowed hard. Squire stared across the water with the fighting light gleaming in his green eyes. Hugh slid his pistol up and down in its holster.

"You stay here, Talbot," Dirk said. "You stay here and cover our backs." It was the best he could think of to keep Talbot out of it.

Talbot put Vick into the stream along with the others. "I can shoot straighter than any of you."

He was too young. He was scared, but no worse than Dirk or Tommy. Dirk thought maybe Hugh and Squire lacked the imagination to see everything that might happen.

Judge Coupland met them at the ferry shanty at the foot of the street, among the cottonwood stumps. "Two men brought those cattle in last night," he said. "Josh Burrage saw the brands and told me. Carmody is stalling about buying the critters."

"Arn and Aaron? They look like brothers?" Dirk asked.

Coupland nodded. He was wearing a pistol. "Right now they're in the River Saloon. I'll go with you."

"No," Dirk said. "Just tell 'em we want to see 'em outside." His voice was flat.

One of the farmers the Breslins had run out of the Breakwagons was standing near Burrage's smithy. "Look at those gun-toting outlaws," he muttered. "Cattlemen."

Dirk said to Burrage: "See that the girls are clear of the street, Josh." He never would be any good as a pistol fighter, Dirk thought, because he was always thinking of something else besides the actual fight.

"Especially that oldest girl," Hugh said,

grinning at Dirk, "the one you got so taken up with when we were having the branding irons made."

Hugh would think of something like that, but his face said that the immediate problem was foremost with him.

"We keep spread apart from each other, see?" Dirk's voice shook.

They got off their horses below the River Saloon. Dirk noticed then that the sun was on the water at their backs. There was a dryness in his mouth and a numbness in his mind.

"Don't we ask about the cattle . . . I mean be sure the two men . . . ?" Tommy Bascomb's voice quavered a little.

"They brought 'em in, didn't they, Judge?" Hugh asked.

Coupland nodded. "Boys, I don't know about this. I've heard those two are the leaders of that northern gang."

"They killed Hull. I know that," Hugh said. "Send 'em out."

The people of the town had caught on now. Merchants were closing doors. Men were ducking behind buildings. Mrs. Burrage ran up the street, calling the names of two of her smallest girls. Her husband bellowed from the smithy that the kids were playing near the river, and then his wife ran down the street again.

"What do we say?" Talbot asked. "What do we say when they come out?"

"Nothing," Dirk said.

"They know," Hugh said.

Judge Coupland walked slowly into the River Saloon. All at once Dirk was thinking of the rainstorm that had come so quickly a long time ago, and of how Pa's face looked as he sang with the water running down his cheeks. All that had nothing to do with the moment, but it came to Dirk and it helped to steady him. He no longer knew whether or not this scene here in the warm street, with the cottonwood stumps still standing before raw buildings, was right or wrong. Now it was something they had come to do, and so they must do it.

The Breslins and the Bascombs were spread across the street, with Dirk and Hugh and Squire in the middle.

"Get farther off, Talbot," Dirk said. "Get over there against that building."

Talbot started to move, and then he stopped.

The two men came out of the saloon quickly. They saw the Breslins and the Bascombs spread out in the street.

"Would you look at that," Arn said. "Pigeons on a fence rail."

Aaron's eyes darted across the line, but his head did not move. "They mean it, Arn." His gaze fixed on Talbot. "Even that white-faced brat that's about to puke has got a gun."

Hugh started it. He went for his pistol. Dirk could not tell afterward what happened. He saw it and he was part of it, but afterwards the blurs of smoke, the noise, and the faces of Arn and Aaron never seemed to separate into the proper sequences. He heard Squire cry out. Dirk was shooting his pistol, aiming and shooting, and sometimes there was so much smoke in front of him and before Arn and Aaron that he was not sure he had a target at all.

His face all at once was numb. He reeled back and fell to his knees, and then he picked his pistol from the dust and shot twice more. The gun was empty then. He was fumbling to reload it when he became aware that there was no noise, except a ringing in his ears. He looked toward Talbot. Talbot was kneeling behind a stump, with his pistol resting on the wood, with both hands on the pistol.

Judge Coupland called from somewhere: "That's all of it, boys!"

Hugh was still erect, his pistol out before him. His face was set and his eyes were pale.

Dirk crawled past his feet to Squire, who was lying on his back, holding his leg.

Dirk used the words he had heard Rusty speak to Brazos: "How bad?"

Squire's mouth worked twice before words came out. "I'm all right. I moved the leg." He was shot through the fleshy part of it, close to the bone.

Dirk rose slowly, afraid of falling. One side of his face was numb. Water was streaming from the eye on that side. Hugh turned his head slowly.

"You got ripped along the jaw, Dirk." Then Hugh yelled: "Talbot! Talbot!"

Talbot was sitting on the stump, throwing up his breakfast.

Hugh swung around, looking straight at Tommy Bascomb. "Tommy! Are you all right?"

Tommy nodded slowly and then, as if he might be wrong, he began to feel his chest and stomach.

Dirk forced himself to walk over and look at Arn and Aaron. They were dead and he knew it at a glance.

"Who got 'em?" Hugh asked.

"They're dead," Dirk said quickly. "Who wants credit for it?" It was in the back of his mind that Talbot, kneeling by the stump, aiming carefully as always, might have got both of them because they did not think him dangerous. Dirk did not want to know who had killed Arn and Aaron.

Judge Coupland was pushing orders in all directions. "Get that wounded boy up to my quarters. Get these two men over on the hill and bury them, and don't put them close to Jake Breslin."

A man clapped Hugh on the shoulder and invited him into the saloon for a drink. Hugh would have gone, but Dirk grabbed his arm.

"What do you think we are?" he asked heatedly. The man was half drunk. Dirk shoved him away.

The farmer who had spoken to the boys when they passed the blacksmith shop now looked at them in awe. For a moment Dirk wanted to explain this thing to him and to explain, also, why it had been necessary to run him out of the Breakwagons. But Dirk knew that there was now a gulf between him and the men who were like the farmer. It was part of the price of being a cattleman. Of trying to defend that right.

After Squire had been taken care of in the judge's quarters, Hugh slipped away to the saloon. Dirk knew it, but he did not bother to go after him. In time Hugh would be fitted completely into the customs of the country, and be as tough as any man out here. Someday he would ride away to look for the man who had killed Pa, and he would find the man and kill him. Dirk knew there was nothing he could do to stop that.

Judge Coupland said: "Some of you had better get back home as fast as you can and tell your folks."

"Talbot, you and Tommy go," Dirk said.

"Tom," the youngest Bascomb said. "I'm getting tired of that Tommy stuff."

Dirk watched his brother and Tommy ford the river. They seemed to ride with a new assurance. From where he stood at the head of the street, they looked like men going about serious business.

Coupland came out while Dirk was standing there uncertainly. "Son, I know just how you feel. I've had to kill three men in my time, and it didn't set easy afterward. Today I was ready to kill two more, if it had to be done. From what I've learned, those two were the real leaders of the hellions north of here. This won't settle everything for you out there in the Breakwagons, but it will help. You'll have more trouble, Dirk, until outlaws know they can't ride over you roughshod." He looked toward the River Saloon. "Try to hold Hugh down all you can. He most likely will never be bad, but he's going to be tough."

Josh Burrage came up the street, wearing his leather apron. The mark of his work lay darkly in the pores of his skin. He addressed his words to Coupland and Dirk as equals. "Them two left horses in my corral, good saddle stock. Fine rigs, too. What'll we do with them?"

Coupland looked at Dirk. "I suppose we could say, with more or less justice, since you and the Bascombs have lost property to the outlaws, that you and Squire are rightfully entitled. . . ."

"No," Dirk shook his head. What the Breslins needed would have to be gained some other way, and he knew it was the same with the Bascombs.

Coupland was pleased. "I would have felt the same way, Dirk. Hold the horses, Josh. We'll sell them and put the money into a school fund. By gosh, yes! We've got to have a school around here right quick. I'll donate the ground, somewhere quite a distance from the saloons. We'd better get a meeting up in a day or two. . . ." He was off again.

Dirk Breslin walked on the hill where his father was buried. It was hard now to recall the things Pa must have dreamed and wanted. Maybe he would have liked cattle, if the chance had come to him that his sons now shared. When he thought about it long enough, Dirk was sure that Pa would have loved the green swells of the Breakwagons.

The first hills were there before Dirk. Cattle country, clean and rich. The Breakwagons seemed to draw in on themselves, as an empire of their own that shut away the vastness around them. Those hills were home now, and any man must fight for his home. Dirk realized that from the day he had taken the lines to put the wagon across the river, he had grown up faster than his years. That had been forced upon him and for a long time he had rebelled against the change, but now he must accept it.

If it took more fighting to hold the Breakwagons, then that must be accepted, too. Out there was the future, but he was no longer afraid of it.

In the spring Rusty would be back, with the bull he had promised. Mostly likely, too, he would bring another drive of mavericks and he would bring, Dirk knew, a crew of men to avenge what had happened at the water hole. If the Texans needed help, it would be ready in the Breakwagons.

Dirk stood a long time on the hill, looking out at home. There were many things that must be done out there, but there was a lifetime to do them.

After a while he began to think of Josh Burrage's oldest daughter, Rachel.

TOWER OF ROCKS

I

Roy Hale was feeling pretty good when he came out of the Mountain House after his visit with Sara Perkins. For the first time since coming West, he saw the promise of a planned future, instead of the catch-as-catch-can existence he had been following.

The board sidewalk that ran only fifty feet each way from the entrance to the hotel was lumpy with the tracked-on mud of hundreds of booted feet. Everyone in Denver was going or coming, bustling, talking loudly. Buckskin mingled with broadcloth. It was a quick, raw, new town, as Hale saw it.

He lit a cigar and leaned against the front of the building, and he wondered if even half of the people on the busy street knew why they were there or what they hoped to accomplish.

But there was a feeling here — enthusiasm, energy, unbounded hope. It seemed to pervade everything about the town, and it was as elemental as the wind from the plains that was beginning to dry the choppy mud of the streets.

Few graybeards were crossing the plains. This was country for the young — the town itself and everything back there in the mountains that ran across the western sky a few miles away.

As he stood watching the pulsing surge of hopeful, energetic people, Hale's expression changed. He was a young man himself, but for a long time there had been a tight-lipped, controlled look of bitterness about him. Now, for a while, he responded to the feeling around him. His square-chinned face with its heavy brows lost its brooding look, and his eyes looked out with almost the same bright eagerness that had been there on a faraway day when, wearing a brand-new gray uniform, he had ridden down the long lane of live oaks with cousin, Scott Morgan, laughing, on their way to join a Virginia company. For just a short time Hale was fully young again.

Then it all came back. It began with the boy. He was a tough-looking youngster with shaggy blond hair spilling out from under a round felt hat with a wide brim. His boots slopped mud as he dodged across the street in front of a heavy freight wagon. The teamster cursed him and cracked his long lash a few inches above the round hat. The boy yelled — "Go to hell!" — thumbed his nose, and then he hit the wall in a skidding jump.

With a fine disregard for other pedestrians, the boy barged through the flow of foot traffic and came straight to Hale. "You're Roy Hale, huh?"

"That's right. Who are you?"

"Ace Cook, since you got to know."

Hale grinned, watching as the boy dug into his pockets. "I had it somewhere," the lad said. His eye fell on Hale's belt buckle. CSA. Confederate States of America. The boy pointed at it, scowling. "One of them, huh? Boy, I sure wouldn't wear that thing if I was you. Pa says all the damned Rebs should've been made to stay down South with the niggers, instead of scattered everywhere with decent people."

There it was again. Hale's expression retreated back to the careful, bitter look. You lost. It was done — that should be enough for the victors. But the bastards had to keep beating you over the head.

Ace Cook found what he was looking for. He handed a note to Hale.

The first few words unlocked memories

that leaped across Hale's mind like fire. "Who gave you this?" he asked.

But the boy was already gone, his boots jetting brown mud as he raced across the street.

Passers-by looked curiously at the tall, grim-faced man staring bleakly at a scrap of paper. It was a land where almost everyone felt free to ask about a man's present business, leaving his past affairs to himself, if he did not care to talk about them. But no one asked Roy Hale what had struck him.

Miners, merchants, trappers, clerks, gamblers, and a hundred others who did not yet know just what they were in a new country — they walked past Hale, and he did not see them, but they saw him, and they did not ask him anything.

He was obviously a man who wanted no kind word from anyone, in spite of the fact that he must have received some terrible news.

The Plains. Pretend you never saw me before. Remember the black horse, Codori house?

It came back in smoke and fire and the thunder of the greatest cannonade ever heard in America. The Southern guns on Seminary Ridge were silent now, many of them dismounted, blown askew by the heavy return fire of the Yankee artillery across the way on Cemetery Ridge. But the Union guns had quit first. It was good to think that they were all knocked out.

In deadly quiet and with unusual military order Hale's company of Virginians rose from behind the stone wall and formed in the pall of smoke. Cousin Scott said quietly: "That clump of trees over there . . . where the smoke is just clearing. We'll drive clear through them and roll them back over the hill."

There was no yelling anywhere along the line.

There were fifty regiments in the massed line, nineteen of them Virginians. The line extended for a mile, but the weight would converge from both ends to drive against the focal point, the clump of trees there on the far ridge where the Yankees waited behind low stone walls.

15,000 men went down from Seminary Ridge, out of the drifting smoke of their now silent artillery. They advanced without shouting or fanfare, smartly aligned as they had never been before in any battle. Strong and steady, a great tide of flashing gun barrels and bayonets, they rolled down the slope through the stifling heat toward the gentle swale where ran the Emmitsburg Road.

Hale looked back at his company. They were walking proudly. Not one full uniform was left among them now. Cousin Scott was wearing a Union officer's hat. It had a wide gray band, a strip of velvet that a girl had stitched to the felt one night when Cousin Scott went visiting in a small town where the regiment had camped during the march into the fat and prosperous land of Pennsylvania.

The brim of the black hat was upswept to a jaunty angle, and fastened to the band was a gay red cockade that bobbed to Cousin Scott's stride. "Follow that red bunny-tail and you'll never lack for a fight," Sergeant Wade had told the company.

Down the slope they went, the foremost hardly breaking stride as they swept the rail fences out of the way. The Emmitsburg Road was close ahead, and beyond was the easy incline up to Cemetery Ridge. Just across the road were the buildings of the Codori farm. It was a name that Hale would never forget. In the almost eerie stillness an order was shouted down the line, and the tempo of the charge increased to a trot.

As they crossed the road, Hale saw an officer on a coal-black horse in the orchard. There was no mistaking the set of the shoulders and head, the auburn curls escaping the tilted hat. General Pickett.

A moment later hell came loose at the hinges. The Union batteries on the ridge were not disabled. The gunners had run them back to cool, and now they had wheeled them back into the cemetery and were serving them with the devilish skill that the blue-bellies always showed with things mechanical.

Hale waved the company on. There was no wavering anywhere in the mass of men who jogged up the hill. Shrapnel was blowing gaps in the line, but the men closed after each bloody shredding, their heads lowered a little, their shoulders hunched, as if they were going against a strong wind. They had never failed against the Army of the Potomac, and they would not fail on this hot afternoon.

From the Roundtops, more than a mile to the right, more shells came screaming in to tear the ground, to maim and kill. Hale cursed the terrible skill of the Union gunners and led his men on up the slope. They were using canister now up there in the cemetery. Hale heard the venomous whizzing of the balls after the casings broke, and he saw men going down by fours and fives.

Through the blue-gray smoke on the ridge he caught glimpses of the busy Yankee gunners. He saw the red belching of the cannon muzzles. Like fiends from some hellish scene that never should have been, the gunners served the pieces, leaping in the smoke and lancing flames.

All the way up the slope the right flank of the Southern line had been angling toward the focal point of trees, knocking down the zigzag rail fences as they went, leaping the low stone walls. The charge was going home. And then from the drifting smoke to the right came a sudden crackle of rifle fire that grew in volume until it settled into a steady, pounding roar. Taken in enfilade, the right flank, where Hale was, began to melt away. A sheet of flame raced across the low stone wall at the top of the ridge.

Some of the artillery was still firing, at almost point-blank range. Again Hale waved his company on. Less than half of the men were left. He saw Cousin Scott swinging his arm, urging them up the slope. The crippling fire from the right never slackened.

The right flank never reached the ridge to overrun the stone wall and grapple with the gunners. Hale saw only a few Virginians who broke in panic and ran back down the hill. The others turned away from an impossible task, still dying as they went down the slope, sullen in defeat, walking away from it in good order.

Although Hale fought on to the end of the

war, it had ended for him that day on the slope below Cemetery Ridge. He did not know until years afterward how decisive the battle had been. Pickett's charge had breached the center of the Union line, but only briefly. Hale did not know that, either, until he got back to Seminary Ridge.

All he knew as he walked away with Cousin Scott, trudging past men in butternut and gray who lay unmoving, stepping around bundles of dirty clothing that writhed and moaned and threshed, was that out of the monstrous violence had come a great weariness of spirit. It was not the dullness of his body that overwhelmed him, or the loss of the battle, but his own rebellion against the hatreds and stupidities that had caused the war.

There, under the ridge he had never reached, Hale had seen Gettysburg as the distillation of everything that was wrong with man. To some extent the thought would lose its sharpness as time passed, and he would go on fighting to the end because there seemed to be nothing else to do.

The firing at the apex of the assault ended before Hale and Cousin Scott reached the Codori house. On Cemetery Ridge the Yankees stood up and gave a long victory shout that rolled down the slope above those who could not hear, and those who were crying out to God and man for help.

Cousin Scott stopped and turned and shook his fist at the shouting. "It's the only time you Yankee sons-of-bitches ever won!"

He saw men grouped around the Codori house. The orchard, some of the trees sill unshattered, was full of more men. "We're rallying for another charge," Cousin Scott said. "And this time. . . ."

It was no rallying point, but a gathering place for the wounded.

The remnant of Hale's company was waiting on the road. Sergeant Wade was not among them. They did not talk as they slogged back up the hill to Cemetery Ridge.

Hale took one long last look at the orchard, remembering how quiet it had been, recalling General Pickett there on his restless black horse. And then he took a deep breath that did not seem to give him any air, and he followed his ragged men up the hill toward the Southern line.

There were times when it all seemed part of a distant past, with the brutal edges smoothed away. Hale would have preferred to keep it that way, but there was no forgetting.

There were thousands left like Ace Cook's pa, and they passed it on to their sons. No, they did not want you to forget. They wanted you to remember that they had won and you had lost.

Hale tore the note into tiny bits and dropped them on the mud-lumped walk and ground the toe of his boot against the pieces, as if the act would bury old memories that he did not want revived.

It had started, though, and it would not stop. Pickett on the black horse in the orchard of the Codori farm. A thousand men had seen him there. Any one of them who had survived could have written the note.

Who had commented about the incident afterward? To whom had he talked at some time, so that the memory was now fixed as a common point of identity? Cousin Scott, yes. That brought up another bitter thought. Cousin Scott had been killed during the retreat to the flooding Potomac. After walking unscathed through the carnage of Pickett's charge, he had been killed by wild shooting from the dark during a Union cavalry foray in the dead of night against Lee's wagons near Monterey in the Blue Ridge Mountains.

Everything was bitterness now. Hale had to remember, too, his going home after the war. The plantation was in ruins, and he found out that both his father and his younger brother had died in the wilderness. His mother had gone north to live with his sister, Evelyn. A year before Fort Sumter, Evelyn had married a Yankee major. He was a brigadier now. Yes, that boy with his damned note had given Hale plenty to think about. Grinding the bits of paper underfoot had not helped at all.

Suddenly Hale stepped out from the wall and walked in the opposite direction from the Plains Saloon. Why talk to some ex-soldier who had nothing better to do than disinter things that Hale wanted to forget?

He walked until he had left the crowds behind and was standing on the bank of Cherry Creek, looking toward the mountains. Men were making fortunes up there, he had heard. There seemed to be something to it, sure enough, for, during the week he had spent in Denver, he had seen gold dust and nuggets dumped rather freely on bars. Some of those tales of wealth to be had for the taking were enough to excite the imagination. Anyone could become a millionaire as soon as he found a good placer gulch. It was odd, though, how many ragged-ass millionaires there were in Denver, men who were waiting out the winter so they could return and make another million.

Sara Perkins did not think much of mining. There were slower but more stable ways to make money, according to her, although she had not yet decided just what her course would be.

From fifty yards away a man peered out at Hale from a sagging, weather-browned tent. He hesitated for a moment, and then he walked down to Hale. "Give her another week or two to melt a little more, and then you can get back to your claim."

"You think a week or two will be enough?"

"Well, it depends a little on where your claim is." There was a young face behind the bushy brown beard. The man's clothes were coming apart. He stood with the raw wind riffling the front of his flannel shirt where buttons were missing, and he looked at the mountains with a rapt expression. "Where is your claim?"

"I've never been any closer to those mountains than I am right now," Hale said.

"The hell! I thought the way you were staring up there. . . . Well, you know. . . ." The man paused. "How about some coffee?"

There was a blackened coffee pot on rocks at the edge of a fire pit in front of the tent. Coals glowed in the pit as the wind swept feathery ashes across their boots. The man's name was Clarence Adams. He told Hale where his claim was, but it meant nothing to Hale. Somewhere there beyond the mountains.

"I wolfed it out one winter," Adams said. "You never saw such snow. My partner died of pneumonia in December or January . . . we'd lost track of the time . . . and then I was alone until spring. No more of that for me, mister. I got out last fall while the getting was good."

"Camped here all winter?"

"Right here. I worked around the saloons a little, helped unload freight, dug a few outhouses for folks . . . I made it through, all right, and now in a week or two I'll be heading back to the hills." Adams studied Hale. "You got a pardner?"

"No, I'm not planning on mining."

"It's the quick way," Adams said. "You make it fast in mining, and then you can light out for home."

Home. Hale put that thought out of his mind as quickly as he could. He liked Adams. There was a pleasant comradeship in standing around a fire drinking coffee with someone who did not insist on talking about the war.

Gettysburg was growing hazy again. Hale was content to let Adams run on about the wonders of placer mining on Beaver Creek, wherever that was.

"We could throw in together, Hale. I won't lie . . . I'm broke. But I've got the claim, and it's a dandy. All we need is a little money for supplies, a good pack horse. . . . By next fall we can come out of there stinking rich!"

"That makes a fine sound, but how can you be sure?"

"You're from the South, ain't you?"

"Yes," Hale said quietly. His mood began to change at once.

"I don't mean anything by asking. Hell, it's all over as far as I'm concerned. I was in the Union navy. I guess we didn't get as stirred up about things as some of the others. You understand what I mean, don't you?"

"Yeah." Hale put his tin cup down by the rock. "Thanks." He walked away.

He had just changed his mind. He was going to the Plains Saloon, after all, to find the man who remembered Pickett on a black horse.

II

Masons were putting a brick front on the Plains Saloon, covering the wide boards of native lumber that were already warped and

115

brown. Inside, it was one long room full of smoke and noise.

The first man Hale saw was Louis Jones, alone at the near end of the long bar, a glass of beer before him. The Negro was a sturdy man of quiet, steady expression. He was wearing high Apache moccasins, a heavy sheepskin coat that did not quite cover the beaded flap below the tip of his holster.

My God, not Louis! How would he have known about the Codori house?

Hale glanced quickly around the room. *Pretend you never saw me before.* There were plainsmen and miners and sharpers and heaven knew who else along that bar. The gambling tables at the back of the room were doing a brisk business.

So far, there was not a man, aside from Louis, who Hale had ever seen before. He still could not believe that Louis had sent the note, but he decided to play the hand out all the way.

Ignoring Louis, Hale stepped up beside him and ordered a beer. He had no use for beer, but a glass of it would enable him to stall until he could spot his man. Studying faces in the mirror, Hale saw no one at the bar who he recognized. He turned to glance casually at Louis. Hale knew him all right.

Louis returned not the least sign of recognition.

Two — no, it was three now — weeks before, they had met on the Smoky Hill Trail. Hale had been guiding two titled Englishmen on a buffalo hunt. It was their first experience with the shaggy animals, and also Hale's, and, since all three of them knew nothing about buffalo hunting, things had worked out pretty well until a small band of determined Cheyennes broke into the scene. One thing about the English, Hale had to admit, they were cool and steady under fire. They lost neither their poise nor their clipped humor while lying behind their dead horses on an open prairie, with seven Indians trying to overrun them.

Squinting down his rifle, Lord Westin had said: "Those naked chaps ride like nothing I've ever seen before. What polo players they'd make, I swear!" He had fired and missed. "Damn the beggars! They won't hold still."

The way Hale had sized it up, the Cheyennes were going to make it stick. They had lost one man in their first sweep around the position, but they had killed both of the pack horses. That had left only one, since Hale had already killed the Englishmen's mounts to make the barricade. As soon as they had settled down, he had figured the Indians would surely realize that one dismounted man on the little chocolate-drop mound about 150 yards away would make the white man's position untenable.

The Cheyennes had skittered their ponies out of rifle range and held a conference. Hale had seen one of them point toward the mound. Not one but two riders had started to circle around to get behind it.

It was then that Louis Jones had come out of the sandhills behind the Indians. He had ridden like a wild man. He had got one man with his pistol as he broke through the group, and he sure as hell had confused the others. With his chestnut at full gallop, he had fired back across the rump of the horse like a Yankee cavalryman with Jeb Stuart on his tail.

Straight up to the dead-horse barricade he had come, dismounting in a flying leap. He then had whipped a rifle from its boot and began to fire at the two Cheyennes who had been heading toward the mound. They soon gave up their idea and had headed back to the main group. With the odds in their favor greatly reduced, the Cheyennes had decided that it was a bad gamble. Standing with one foot on his dead horse, Lord Westin had saluted them as they rode away. Hale had stared at Louis. He had not wanted to believe that a Negro could ride like that.

Two days later, with Hale's horse packing two buffalo heads that the Englishmen absolutely had refused to give up, the party had fallen in with Sara Perkins's wagon train. For a price, Louis had ridden back by night and retrieved the Englishmen's saddles.

It had taken a week to get on into Denver. During that time Hale had listened to Louis's story in scraps and fragments. Born in slavery, Louis had run away after one week as a field hand, three years before the war.

"Mister Lincoln's Emancipation Proclamation must have relieved your mind a great deal," Lord Hughes had commented.

Louis had looked at him quietly. "He didn't free me. I figure I was born free."

He was a bounty hunter, Louis Jones, a man who made a practice of securing a deputy's commission from a sheriff in a county where a reward stood on the head of a man who had fled a crime. Armed with such a commission and a warrant — usually for murder — a bounty hunter was free to accomplish just as much as he had the guts to do. Hundreds of miles from where

119

his commission bore any weight at all, he still had a warrant that any honest law official was obliged to respect. When a bounty hunter cornered a fugitive, the hard way was to take him alive and return him all the way to the state and county of the crime. A simpler way was to kill him, wherever found, and preserve substantial evidence of the death in order to collect the reward.

Despicable as the profession of bounty hunting was, it was a way to make a living if a man had a strong stomach. As for Louis in particular, Hale's view of him was colored by the circumstances of their first meeting. When the two Englishmen had wanted to reward Louis for what he had done, he had looked at them scornfully and said: "Just for saving your bacon?"

"Bacon?" The lords exchanged confused looks, and Hale had to explain.

The night before Sara Perkins's wagons had reached Denver, Louis had disappeared. Here in the saloon was the first Hale had seen of him since.

On Hale's right was a burly man in a buffalo coat. The looks and smell of him proclaimed bullwhacker. His dark beard was matted with dried mud and blood, and there were recent cuts and bruises on his face. He appeared to have been in a brawl a short time before, and the red meanness in his eyes said he was ready to go again.

"You don't much give a damn who you drink with, do you?" he asked Hale, and then looked past him at Louis.

Hale sipped his beer. He looked the bullwhacker over carefully and said: "Now that you mention it, sir, I do care."

While the man was straining to answer through the whiskey vapors in his head, Hale took his beer glass and walked away. As he moved along behind the men at the bar, Hale rechecked his first survey of faces. It came out the same. From the belligerent bullwhacker with the cuts on his ugly face to the other end of the bar, there was no one Hale knew.

He wandered on back to the gambling tables. For a few moments he thought that one of the sharp-eyed dealers resembled closely a major he had known from Longstreet's division. Then the man said: "All right, friends, let's look at the next beautiful card in the box." His accent was as New England as a keg of codfish.

For a while Hale watched a faro bank game where a drunken youngster with a wispy beard was making impossible bets. He whooped each time he lost. "Plenty more where that came from, boys!"

Hale observed that some of the "boys" were taking a narrow-eyed interest in the youth and his seemingly inexhaustible supply of gold pieces.

Again Hale saw no one he knew. Then it must be Louis. Still, Hale was not ready to accept that as a fact. Perhaps his man had been here earlier and left, or maybe he had not arrived yet.

As Hale turned away, he bumped into the stocky man whose arm was in a sling. "I beg your pardon."

The man smiled. "No harm done, sir." He held Hale's gaze for a long moment before moving closer to the gamblers.

The accent started it. The long look was another sharp stick that prodded memory. Before he reached the end of the bar, a tiny floodgate opened in Hale's mind and poured out the small details of remembrance.

With his back to the bar, Hale sipped at his lukewarm beer and studied the man. One of the Tidewater Blaines with the Biblical names. Right! Captain Ezekiel Blaine. Why, he and Hale had campaigned together for almost a year. A few months before Gettysburg, Blaine had been transferred to Garnett's brigade. The man was changed. He had been thin and wiry, with a sharp face and eyes full of the devil, a flashing white-toothed grin, always a gambler with money, women, or his own life. Now he was heavy, his face full and no longer burned by wind and sun to a hard, lean brown.

We're all changed, Hale thought. *We have a right to be changed. Now, what was the next step? What was so almighty confidential that Blaine had to go through a mysterious rigmarole just to talk to an old friend? Well, let Blaine make the move.*

It came soon enough.

The youngster who had been making the outrageous bets at faro bank won twice in a row. He shouted for everyone to belly up to the bar. A moment later Hale heard the bullwhacker's voice raised in drunken anger against Louis. Apparently already a loser, that bullwhacker did not know what he was letting himself in for, Hale thought grimly. Hale had seen Louis move with the effortless grace of a cat one morning when a horse broke its halter and wheeled to run. He had seen Louis use his fists, too. It was surprising, then, that Louis suddenly gave way before the man's abuse and went across the room to take a chair against the wall.

The winning gambler was shouting, shaking a handful of gold coins over his head. He was drunk and foolish enough to be taken home, spanked by his mother, and put to bed.

During the shuffling and confusion while men were crowding up to the bar, Blaine paused beside Hale. "Back door in about ten minutes, Roy." Blaine was smiling, looking elsewhere as he spoke, and then he stepped away from Hale and shouted: "Name your libation, gentlemen! We've got a lucky winner here today. The next one will be on the house!"

"You, too, boy!" the winner yelled, shaking his fistful of gold at Louis. Two of the coins fell to the floor, and the youth took a swaggering kick at them. "A tip for the swamper!"

One of Sara Perkins's teamsters had called Louis "boy" just once too often. On a brisk dawn when tempers were not at their best anyway, Louis had knocked the man kicking over a wagon tongue. But from the drunken youngster, Louis took the word impassively. He held up his glass of beer, as if to say: "Thanks, but I've already got a drink."

It was good enough for the youth but not good enough for the bullwhacker, who lurched over in front of Louis and said: "Now you're too good to drink with us, huh, you black bastard!"

That was a huge lump to swallow. Hale did not expect it to go down, but Louis smiled slowly. "You just told me to get away from the bar. Make up your mind."

"If there's one thing I can't stand, it's a smart nigger, especially one that thinks he's man enough to wear a pistol. What do you figure to do with that thing, boy?"

Two men, either friends of the bullwhacker or at least sharing his attitude, joined the first one. Even sober, they would not win much from Louis in a rough-and-tumble brawl, Hale figured. They had him front and flanks, with his back to the wall, and he was still sitting.

Hale knew how he could move, however. He fully expected to see Louis explode from the chair and floor the bullwhacker in the buffalo coat before the man knew what had hit him. In fact, Hale was relishing the thought. But it was not going to be that way. One of the men was reaching into his pocket for a pistol.

"Boys, would you say that we're getting too many blackbirds out here these days?" the bullwhacker asked.

"Yeah!"

There had been a quick sliding away of men from the bar. Some of them got in Hale's way as they streamed toward the back of the room. He shouldered two of them aside with his sudden movement to get into the clear. "Leave him alone," he said.

The three men swung around. "What kind of a nigger-lover are you?" one of them asked.

"Find out."

It seemed to Hale that it hung too long. They were mean enough and drunk enough to try it. Louis must have thought the same way, for suddenly he drew his pistol.

Then Blaine said calmly: "Let's not have any trouble, gentlemen." He was standing behind the bar. A shotgun rested on the wood, and he was holding it with one hand. Two loud clicks sounded.

It was all over then. The bullwhacker saved what face he could. "By God, boys! A den of nigger-lovers. Let's take our business somewhere else."

"Please do, gentlemen," Blaine said pleasantly.

The three men stumbled out, cursing the Plains and everyone in it. There was a rush back to the bar, and loud talk rose again. Blaine gave the shotgun to a bartender. "Uncock that damned thing, will you?" Someone who did not believe in tips for swampers scooped up the two coins on the floor.

Louis Jones sat staring at Hale. His look plainly said: "I didn't need any help from you."

A man paid his debts, Hale thought, even to a black bounty hunter who accepted payment with a sullen look.

A few minutes later Hale went out to keep his appointment in the back room.

III

"It's been a long time, Roy." Ezekiel Blaine shook his head. "You haven't changed much, though. I knew you the minute I saw you."

"When was that?"

"This morning. You were just going into the Mountain House. I almost yelled at you from across the street, and then the idea hit me."

"What idea?"

Blaine smiled. "We'll get to that. First I'd like to catch up on a little ancient history."

There must be a double partition between the combination office and living quarters where they were and the saloon proper, Hale thought. He could hear the sounds from the barroom only indistinctly. "You live here?" he asked, looking around at the

127

Spartan simplicity of the room.

"Part of the time, yes." Blaine raised his head to forestall comment. "I know, I know. I used to do better even in the Army."

Hale smiled. "You certainly did." Blaine had been the envy of the whole brigade because he always managed to secure comfortable quarters, sumptuous meals, and other luxuries even under the most trying circumstances. And, as far as it would go, he had always shared everything with his fellow officers.

"What have you been up to since the war?" Blaine asked.

Hale shrugged. He gave a brief history of his activities — deputy sheriff in Texas, railroad worker, cowboy, wanderer. He did not mention his last venture as a guide.

"Your family . . . how are they?"

"My mother and my sister are in Ohio," Hale said curtly. "They're all that's left."

"I'm sorry." Blaine rose and got a bottle of whiskey and glasses from a cupboard. He poured the drinks. "Damnation to old Abe's bones."

Hale did not care for the toast, and he did not want to talk about the war. "What's on your mind, Ezekiel?"

"I'll get to it." Blaine walked slowly around the room. "I've still got the old place

128

in Virginia. It was a hell of a thing to pay the taxes they laid on it, but I've managed to do it. One day, before long, I'm going back, and then I'll. . . ." He stared at Hale. "Well, I'm going back."

The change was much deeper than his physical appearance, Hale realized. There was a bitterness in him that glinted from his eyes, a hard set to his mouth that spoke of long-nurtured anger. There was no going back for any man. They all talked about it, but Hale knew it would not work.

Blaine poured another drink and gulped it down. "South America, Mexico . . . that's no good. I have a lot of friends who went there." He jabbed his finger at Hale. "Not me. I'm going back and fight them on their own ground."

Suddenly his whole mood changed. He shrugged and sat down, shaking his head. "Wild talk, Roy. We both know it. I guess just seeing you again and thinking of old times touched me off. I can see you don't give a damn to talk about something we can never recover, so let's get down to business." Now there was a cold crispness in Blaine's manner. For a moment he listened to the muted noise of the saloon. "You saw that young idiot in there throwing his gold around?"

Hale nodded.

"Spanish Creek. He's the first man I know of to get out this spring. He came by way of Big Bayou, of course. How the hell he ever lived to make it, I'll never know. He doesn't realize how stupid-lucky he was."

"Bad snow, you mean?"

"Yes, there's still snow on that route, but that's not what I'm talking about. Spanish Creek is the richest placer diggings since California Gulch, maybe even better. I struck it there myself last summer. That's how I got this place." Twisting to his left to open a desk drawer, Blaine bumped his right elbow. He grimaced in pain and rubbed the elbow through the sling. "I wish that damned thing would get well." From his desk he took a small, beautifully drawn map. The larger details had been painted in watercolors. He let Hale study it for two minutes. That was more than enough time for Hale to get the feel of Spanish Creek out there between two mountain ranges.

"Terrible Pass . . . is that really twelve thousand feet high?"

Blaine nodded. "At least that. Have you ever been in high mountain snow?"

"Not even in high mountains without snow. I don't know what you're working up to, but already I don't like the looks of it."

Blaine laughed. "Cautious old Roy, but when it called for boldness, you didn't lack for that, either. Such a rare combination is exactly what I need now."

"I'm not so sure about that. You haven't even come close to the point yet."

"I'll get there. Have another drink."

"No, thanks."

"*I* will then." Blaine stared at Hale over the glass. "Do you know that you're the first man I've seen from Kemper's brigade since the war? It means a great deal to me, Roy. Oh, I know . . . look to the future, bind up the wounds, join in holy brotherhood with the Yankee bastards. Sure, I've tried all that, and maybe even a little of it stuck, but I've also stared into a lot of lonely campfires half the night, fighting the whole thing over again."

"I know what you mean."

Blaine put his glass down and cupped his free hand, palm up. "We had it right in our grasp that first day at Gettysburg. It slipped away from us through no one's fault." The unquenched flame of the old loss gleamed in his eyes. "We had it again on the third day. We could have ended the whole thing right there if Uncle Robert had thrown thirty thousand men against their center instead of half that many. By God, we would have won!"

Hale picked up the bottle. "I'll drink to that." Not for a long time had he given way to what-might-have-been. It was not easy to be a Southerner in 1868. Although anything they could say now was only momentary insulation from the harsh fact that they were losers, they could at least find fleeting comfort in sharing the loss.

Some of the roundness of Blaine's face was whiskey bloat, but for a short time Hale could remember him flat-cheeked, laughing, devil-may-care, like Cousin Scott and thousands of others on the silent roster of the Confederacy.

The whiskey helped, although Hale knew it was no solution, for after a time he would have to leave the quiet room and resume his life among the victors. "Garnett's brigade went right past the Codori house?"

Blaine nodded.

They talked then of things that Hale had pushed aside for a long time. He lost track of time. In the end it was Blaine who came around again to Spanish Creek.

"Since late last summer I've been running a gold express from the mining camps. No man has lost one ounce of any shipment entrusted to me. On delivery here at the bank, I collect ten percent of the full amount. So far, it's been too simple to believe. I've been lucky. Small shipments, I'll admit, but not the least trouble." Blaine paused, rubbing his elbow, studying Hale keenly. "But now it's Spanish Creek. I've got three good men, but for Spanish Creek I need a special kind of man. That's why I'm offering you a thousand dollars to be the courier. It may not sound like much, but there's one big item to consider. I guarantee delivery. In case of loss, I pay off at eighty percent."

"What's the total at Spanish Creek?"

"Possibly thirty-five thousand dollars. You'll have to check it."

"I don't know the first thing about gold."

"You really don't have to. You'll be dealing with honest men. You ought to know exactly the amount you're handling, but if it's impossible. . . ." Blaine spread his hands.

Hale picked up the bottle. It was getting rather light. "I take it that not everyone in Spanish Creek is honest?"

Blaine grunted. "Two Southerners found that place. Then the others came in . . . bounty jumpers, Northern white trash of all kinds. They organized the district and in the process shoved our men up a little branch creek that they thought was worthless.

"I came along later with four others. We threw in with the other Southerners. One claim was just beginning to look good, but nobody really knew what was on any of the claims. We threw in together, share and share alike, to work all the ground. The owner of that one claim didn't come in because he was doing pretty well. We hit it, Hale. That little branch turned out to be the richest place in the whole gulch. They say a man never quits when he finds gold, but I did. I took my share, sold out to the others, and came here. I was lucky to get away. Not very many others have since late summer. That young fool out there at the faro bank table is the first one I know of this spring. Men tried it. Some of the bodies were found less than a mile from camp, others part way up Terrible Pass, and no telling how many more haven't been found. Now Steve Munson and his men are caught in the middle of it, with a fortune in gold."

In spite of the whiskey, Blaine's eyes were clear and his voice unslurred. He rested his good arm on the table and gave Hale a long, serious look. "I wanted you to know that it won't be one of your Sunday picnics with the girls down on the Potomac."

"I'm beginning to see that," Hale said dryly. "What you don't seem to understand is that I haven't taken your job."

"You will, I'm sure. Damn it, Roy, those are Southerners over there, men like you and me!"

"Why don't they take their gold and march out in a group? How many of them are there?"

"Six. They can't make a fast run for it. There isn't a horse or mule left alive in the gulch."

Hale took a fresh cigar from a box on the desk. "How do you know that?"

"Billy Lowe, the young loudmouth in there with all the dust."

"Six men could pack that gold," Hale said.

"Sure, they could. And there's fifteen men, or more, just waiting for them to make that very move. How far do you think Munson and the others would get?"

"Why didn't they get out last summer when you did?"

"They talked about it," Blaine said, "but they couldn't walk away from their rich claims. I offered to send a courier in, but they voted against it. Then the first storm caught them and they were stuck for the winter. By sticking together they've been able to protect themselves and their gold. They're still all right, but their time is running out fast."

"Why? They made it through the winter."

As Hale remembered him, Ezekiel Blaine had never been a patient man. But he was patient now in the face of Hale's questions.

"As soon as travel becomes easy, Spanish Creek will be swarming with people," Blaine said. "If Munson and his boys could hold out that long, they could recruit men to help them. There are plenty of decent people out here, Roy. On the whole, the mining camps have been well regulated by the miners themselves. Spanish Creek is a bad exception. It just happened that Aaron Bliffert wound up there. He organized a group of thugs and murderers from men who ordinarily might not have been any worse than petty thieves. By the time enough decent miners get into that gulch, Bliffert will have to get out or be hanged." Blaine shook his head. "That will be much too late to do our bunch any good.

"If we don't get that gold out for them before the snow goes, Munson's bunch will have to make the try. If they don't, Bliffert will go after it right in camp."

"He had a whole winter to try that last move," Hale said. "Why didn't he?"

"And kill the goose that was laying the golden eggs? Munson's boys were mining all winter, Roy. They couldn't get out.

Besides, there are other men over there who aren't on either side, and they would be witnesses to out-and-out murder. What Bliffert is hoping, I'm sure, is that the Southerners will try to run for it. Then his men will nail them somewhere on a lonely trail. No witnesses. So they don't run, say. Bliffert will be forced to try it the hard way, witnesses or not."

Hale did not like the sound of any of it, except the thousand dollars. "How did this Billy Lowe get out?"

"You're thinking that maybe he's one of Bliffert's men. So did I at first. I never talked to him directly. I just listened to him shooting his mouth off to anyone in range. He came out through Big Bayou. From what he's said, I gather that he was lost most of the time. The fact that he never followed the trail may have saved him. Then, too, he left Spanish Creek at night, in the middle of a spring storm that lasted two days."

For a while the two men were silent, listening to the faint sounds from the saloon.

"You guarantee eighty percent payment on a lost shipment?" Hale asked. Blaine nodded, and Hale went on: "Could you stand it if the Spanish Creek gold was lost?"

"I'd be wiped out, and then some," Blaine

137

said quietly.

"Then the safe thing to do is not to tackle it."

"The cowardly thing, you mean. Those men are Southerners!"

"You've made that point about a dozen times, Ezekiel, so stop hammering me with it. I've seen plenty of Southerners I had no use for."

Blaine was outraged. "What kind of talk is that?"

"I'm not referring to Munson's men. I don't. . . ."

"Not enough money for you?"

"It's plenty. It's just that I. . . ."

". . . don't like the job. Is that it?"

"I haven't said so . . . yet." Hale scowled. "What makes you think I can do something that six men can't do for themselves?"

"The only way it can be done is by one man . . . or a lot of men, which I haven't got and can't get. Deception. Boldness. Caution. You're a master of all three. On top of that, you're so damned honest it hurts."

"Am I?" Hale growled. "How do you know what's happened inside me since the war?"

Blaine smiled slowly. "I'm willing to bet everything I have on what I think didn't happen. Why did you stand up for that black bounty hunter in there?"

"I had my reasons. What were yours?"

"Several," Blaine said. "One is enough, and that was the fact that you had a good chance to get killed. But you acted from a sense of justice. No, you haven't changed one bit, Roy. Will you take the job?"

Hale frowned. He wondered if the whiskey was warping his judgment. "Well, I'd have to know a lot more about it than I do now."

"That's why you and I are here."

A half hour later Hale went out by the back door. He was surprised to find that dusk had come already. At six o'clock he was to have met Sara Perkins for dinner.

Stumbling over evil-smelling piles of garbage, Hale stayed in the alley for almost a block, turning back to the street through a narrow passage between two buildings. Foot traffic had thinned considerably. He paused for a few moments in the shadows, looking both ways on the street before he stepped out and headed for the Mountain House. He had not gone far when he heard someone coming behind him. He stopped by a recessed doorway, waiting.

Louis Jones came out of the dusk unhurriedly. Before he reached the doorway, he said quietly — "Good evening, Hale." —

and then he walked on past.

"Just a minute there, Louis."

Louis stopped. "Yes?" There was a hint of amusement in his voice.

"What's the idea of following me?"

"Well, now, I wouldn't want anything to happen to the man who saved my life from those terrible bullwhackers, would I? Especially when he's drunk."

"Who's drunk?"

Louis's teeth flashed whitely in the gloom. "I beg your pardon. Maybe it was someone else I heard making all that racket in the alley." He walked away.

Sara Perkins was alone at a table in the dining room of the Mountain House. As Hale went toward her, he glanced down at the sorry condition of his boots and pant legs. He straightened his coat and smoothed his hair with his hand.

"Sara, I must apologize. I was. . . ."

"Yes, I see. What time is it, Mister Hale?" She was a cool, self-possessed woman. If there had been just the least hint of fragility about her, she would have been beautiful. Her hair was raven-black, her eyes dark blue. The weather of the plains crossing had turned her skin a soft brown, without any apparent coarsening.

Still standing, Hale made a ritual of taking out his watch. It was a memento of his grandfather on the Upton side. During the war it had run faithfully, somewhat erratically, but at least within a half hour of accuracy in a day. And then at 5:23 a.m. of the day that Uncle Robert rode into Appomattox to see Grant, the ancient turnip had stopped. Hale had wound it with the tiny gold key, but the hands had never moved again. Someday, he thought, he would have it repaired, but he had never done it.

He bowed and said: "It is now five twenty-three, Miss Perkins. I'm early."

His attempts at humor fell flat. "Sit down," Sara said. "I assume you haven't eaten." All that was left before her was a cup of coffee.

As he took a seat, Hale saw Louis enter. Sara looked across the room and nodded, and Louis gave her a little bow. "Shall I invite him to sit with us, Mister Hale?"

Sometimes it was hard for Hale to tell whether she was serious or whether she was gigging him. He was still trying to determine which it was this time, when she said: "Very well, I'll talk to him later."

"Why?"

"Because I want to hire him."

A waiter who sniffed moistly came to the table. "We've got venison and buffalo left.

No more potatoes." He dragged air into his nose and looked with disapproval at Louis, now seated at the first table near the door.

"Buffalo steak, rare," Hale said.

The waiter sniffed again. "We got roast, and it's already cooked."

When he left, Sara said: "I wish someone would give him a handkerchief."

"Potatoes . . . now there's a venture you might try," Hale said. "I heard about a man who raised potatoes and made a fortune selling them in mining camps."

Sara sipped her coffee. "I think they made this from the peelings." She studied Hale sharply. "Did you go to see Ezekiel Blaine?"

"I was in his saloon, yes. Are you keeping track of me?"

"Yes. If you're going to be my right-hand man, I feel obliged to know what your other business interests are."

Hale felt himself bristling. She was acting as if she owned him, prodding into his affairs like that.

"Did you know Mister Blaine before coming here?" she asked.

"Perhaps."

"Do you know what he does now?"

"He runs a saloon," Hale said curtly.

"And an express from the gold fields. That was something that I considered myself, before changing my mind."

She had changed her mind several times, Hale knew. The second night they were together in Denver, he had agreed to work for her, although she never had decided exactly what the venture would be. She had inherited money from the sale of a buggy factory in Indiana. For some time before her uncle's death, she had run the factory herself, doing very well with government contracts for gun caissons.

Her Yankee competence had irked Hale at times. He was damned well irked by it now. If he hadn't known the soft, warm side of her, blessed if he wouldn't tell her simply that he had decided not to work for her and let it go at that. Then she could guess all she wanted to about his business with Blaine. She had just about guessed it already, he thought, and now she would try to pin him down. What was he going to tell her about his reasons for quitting?

The sniffling waiter brought the buffalo roast and thumped it down in front of Hale.

"Would you bring me a small glass of brandy, please?" Sara asked.

"Yes, ma'am!" As an afterthought the waiter asked: "Anything for him?"

Sara smiled. "I think he's had enough."

That was insult enough, but the smirk on

the waiter's face was too much. "Go blow your nose," Hale growled.

"*Tsk, tsk!* Sometimes I don't think you're a Southern gentleman at all."

"I can still order my own whiskey, or not order it, as I please."

"Yes, Mister Hale."

The waiter was a long time in serving Louis, who bore the delay without the least expression of resentment. It was a stupid Northern myth about Negroes having inexhaustible patience simply because they were Negroes, Hale thought. If the waiter discovered that fact the hard way, it would serve him right.

A group of well-dressed men, who obviously had been celebrating at some bar, came in with loud and boisterous talk. They took a table in the center of the room, and the waiter came skipping up to them immediately.

Looking at Louis and speaking to be heard all over the room, one of the roisterers said: "You know it wasn't just a political proclamation when you see them eating in the same room with you."

The second speaker did not look at Hale when he laughed and said: "And the Southern aristocrats will get the good-looking women. What the hell did *we* win?"

Louis's expression did not change. Hale held his temper. He felt drawn to Louis because of the attitudes they both had to endure. They were outcasts, each in his own way.

"You bear up under it very well, Roy," Sara said.

"Sometimes."

There was a softness in her smile now instead of sharp amusement. Hale was "Roy" again. And she had not driven through ruthlessly to pin him down about his talk with Ezekiel Blaine. "I've got to tell you something, Sara."

She waited.

Hale glanced around the dining room. "Not here. May I come up later?"

One thing about Yankee women, at least this one — there was no silly skirmishing before decision, no puerile bantering and gracious-me-how-you-do-carry-on simpering. Sara Perkins looked at Hale steadily and nodded.

Before she left the dining room to go upstairs, she went over to talk to Louis. Hale saw Louis shake his head several times. The bounty hunter was the only one who did not let his dinner stand in order to watch the woman all the way to the lobby door.

Hale had lost all track of women's fashions

during the war. He could not have said whether or not Sara Perkins's clothes were in the latest mode, but he knew that she was a striking figure. She would have made a stir in the ballroom of any mansion he had ever seen.

Feeling in need of at least four hours' more sleep, Hale came downstairs the next morning in the gray light of dawn. The desk clerk was sound asleep in a chair. Hale left payment for his room on the counter. He took time to drink three cups of coffee in a Chinese restaurant, where the bloodshot eyes of the proprietor reminded him of eggs broken in a frying pan.

An hour later he was several miles closer to the snowy mountains. A lone man on a horse, without camping gear or tools. He did not look much like a prospector, but he would make the change when he got to Silver Bell.

The sun came up and warmed his back.

Being a poor liar had its drawbacks, Hale mused. If you could not lie convincingly under certain circumstances, then you ought to keep your mouth shut. But he had failed at both last night with Sara.

Before he had left her, she had gotten the whole story out of him. She knew where he

146

was going and why. His ego kept him from believing that she had given him that little nod solely for the purpose of getting him to blab like a child.

Last night it had been easy to talk, even to brag a little. Today he wished he had kept his big mouth shut.

IV

The road wandered through a break in a sharp-spined hogback that made a definite separation of plains and mountains. Hale overtook two freight wagons that were double-teaming a rocky hill where it seemed no wagon could possibly go. He called a question to the busy teamsters. "Is this still the way to Silver Bell?"

"Hell, yes!" a man yelled. "Uphill both ways."

Soon afterward Hale was riding beside a brawling stream in a cañon that was pinched tight by plunging hills. Wherever there was dirt in the road, he saw the marks of recent travel. He passed a few camps of miners, their sluices set close to the creek in places where gravel had accumulated. It was his first look at placer mining. He could not say much for what he saw. Picking cotton for a living would be better.

The steep walls of the cañon made him

uneasy. He kept looking up, expecting massive rocks to fall. Plenty of them had fallen, almost choking the cañon in places. The excuse of a road twisted among them on a line of least resistance. The farther Hale was, the more convinced he was that he was not going to fall in love with the mountains.

When he reached Silver Bell, he was cold, his stomach was growling with hunger, and he was sour from lack of sleep the night before. The cañon had widened into a respectable valley, and the mountains on both sides were no longer looking straight down the back of his collar.

The town was built as hard astride the creek as tents could be pitched and shacks could be crowded. The orange blobs of lanterns under canvas, the cooking fires in front of tents, and the groups of men around them brought back memories of war bivouacs. But even in war things had been more orderly than this strung-out mess.

Hale rode on toward what appeared to be a more substantial part of the town. Under a lantern above a sign on a log structure he saw Saloon. Under that word, Hotel had been added as an afterthought. The guest-receiving part of the operation was a small counter of rough pine near one wall. The rest of the room was given over to a bar and gambling tables, where business was in full, noisy swing.

Standing before a scowling, red-haired man at the counter was Louis Jones.

Hale stared at him bleakly. *I've had just about enough of his trailing me everywhere I go,* he thought.

"We ain't got a room left," the clerk was telling Louis. "Try Clint Aiken's livery stable. If he won't let you sleep there . . . it's a warm night."

The hell it was, Hale thought. He had been chilled to the bone for the last two hours. He strode up to the counter and said: "I say you've got a room."

The red-headed man caught his accent. "You're not in Charleston now, Reb. I'm running this here place."

"Run it. All we want is rooms, and I happen to know for a fact that you've got them."

"Oh, it's 'we' now, huh?" The clerk looked Louis and Hale over with insulting slowness. Suddenly one side of his mouth curled in a sardonic grin. He pointed at Louis. "First door on the right. It's unlocked. One buck on the counter now."

Louis took out a dollar. With infinite slowness he placed it on the counter. "There you are, my good man."

The clerk's face turned vicious. "I think

149

I'll throw your black ass out in the street right now. In fact. . . ." He started to brush the dollar to the floor.

Hale slapped the man's hand aside. "Shut up and give me a room."

For a moment it was touch and go, the clerk glaring at Louis, and then he looked at Hale, and the corner of his mouth lifted again. "You just gave your *friend* there the last bed in the place. Of course, if he's willing, maybe he'll share it with you." He looked around the room, as if hoping that someone in the noisy place had heard and could share the joke with him.

Louis had started toward the doorless hallway. He paused, looking at Hale, waiting for him to make his decision.

"For four bits you can sleep on one of the tables over there," the clerk said. "That is, after we close the place . . . generally around two o'clock." He laughed.

It had been a sorry day, Hale thought. He put a dollar on the counter and followed Louis.

It was a sorry room, too. There was barely space for the bed, which was no more than a stained ticking stuffed with hay, supported on a framework of poles and rope. One filthy, rumpled blanket. With Hale and Louis both in the room, the place was badly overcrowded.

"Why are you following me?" Hale demanded.

Louis gave him a calm look. "I think I was here first." Louis took his gun belt off and tossed it on the bed. "That Aiken . . . you'll find him in there at the wheel of fortune. He takes the dollar. You take your own horse to the livery stable. No oats. I looked everywhere."

"I want to get something straight with you right now, Louis."

"You got your business. I've got mine. If we happen to ride in the same direction, that's chance. I'm not asking you any questions, Hale."

Louis was not going to answer any questions, either, Hale knew. He went out to take care of his horse.

The washstand, Hale discovered on his return from the stable, was on a stump behind the hotel. Louis had gotten a bucket of hot water from somewhere, and, stripped to the waist in the biting air, he was sloshing and scrubbing vigorously. Hale shivered as he watched him.

Louis took a towel from his pack and began to dry himself. "Hot water in the bucket. The wash pan is nailed to the stump. Must be thieves around here. You've got to whoosh the water out with your hand."

So, whooshing water from the pan, Hale got himself fairly wet. He washed his face and hands and let it go at that.

"Here's the towel if you want it," Louis said.

Hale hesitated.

"The black don't rub off. You ought to know that."

"Don't be so damned smart," Hale growled. "Are those your two mules in the stable?"

"They are. The mining outfit is locked in the little room at the back of the stable. You couldn't see that."

"So you're going mining?"

"Everybody gets rich at it, I hear." Louis laughed.

They ate together in the kitchen behind the barroom. It was elk stew, no vegetables, but plenty of grease and flour gravy that congealed around the edges of the plate.

It was Ezekiel Blaine's idea that Hale outfit in Silver Bell. Prices were higher there, he said, but the idea was that no one would think Hale was headed for a distant mining gulch if he rode away with nothing but saddlebags.

It was food that was worrying Hale more than any other part of what he had to buy in the morning. No potatoes at the Mountain House in Denver. In Silver Bell no one would know what a fresh vegetable was. "You know, no matter how remote and rough a place is, a man deserves a decent meal now and then."

Louis smiled. "Raid a Union supply train."

"You're just full of wise sayings, aren't you?"

After the meal Hale stayed in the saloon long enough to find out a few things that would facilitate his movements in the morning. No one had been over Terrible Pass since the fall before, he was told, and anyone who tried it this early was a pure damned fool. The big strike on Spanish Creek wasn't half of what it was cracked up to be, a man said. A man who wanted to do some real mining ought to go on up the valley to Chimney Rock. It turned out that the informant had a few claims for sale up that way. Although it was very rich ground around Chimney Rock, the man had been forced to come to Silver Bell to rest up and gamble a little because of a bad back.

When Hale went to his room, Louis was sitting on the bed, reading by candlelight. It was the first that Hale had known that Louis could read. A system had been destroyed, but the attitudes still lingered. Hale had been part of the system, and now he found a vague resentment in the fact that Louis was literate.

"What have you got there, Louis?"

"Some of the dialogues of Plato on tyranny."

"Yeah? I suppose you think nothing has changed since his time."

"Yes, I do think that."

"*You're* a free man."

"I'm an exception. I was always free."

"And plenty biggety about it, too," Hale said.

Louis closed the book. He yawned. "Take the outside of the bed, if you want it." He did not leave much choice. He got against the wall, pulled part of the blanket over him, and was asleep in a few minutes.

Lying beside him later, Hale tried to find an answer to why it was so different now. On summer nights beyond counting he had slept with Barry and Larry, Aunt Etta's twins, in the slave cabin behind the big house. They had played together, argued, and fought, and Aunt Etta had smacked them all at times to settle things. He could recall her face more clearly now than the features of anyone in his own family except Cousin Scott. Tall and thin, her graying hair tied back in a knot, Aunt Etta had run the

kitchen of the mansion with a keen competence and sharp impatience for adult error,
but children, black or white, seeking escape
from impending punishment for minor
misdeeds, always knew that Aunt Etta's
kitchen was a haven and that she was a stout
defender of young ones.

No matter how fondly he looked back on
Aunt Etta and her family, Hale knew the
gulf had always been there, widening between him and the boys as they all grew up.
It was not slavery that caused it. Hale's
father had freed all of Aunt Etta's family
when Barry and Larry were twelve. That
had not changed anything. Slavery had been
only a system. White-over-black was an attitude, and it was so deeply ingrained in
Hale that he had a hard time going to sleep,
simply because he was in bed with a Negro.

The building was quiet and the room was
cold when Hale wakened sometime later.
The dark reaches of the night were the
worst possible time to wrestle with an
abstract problem, but again he found himself struggling with the social implications
of sleeping with a black man. He rose and
put on his boots.

Louis had not stirred, but, as Hale was
going out, Louis said softly: "It rubbed off,
after all."

Angered at himself as well as Louis, Hale said: "Go to hell."

The saloon was dead quiet. Hale stretched out on one of the gaming tables and tried to sleep. He did not do very well, but he finally did fall into sound sleep — and then someone began to drag chairs around.

Hale roused up irritably. One of the lamps was burning, and a swamper was cleaning up. "Go on and sleep," the man said. "I won't have to move that table."

"What time is it?"

"About five. Don't mind me." The swamper knocked a chair over and nearly tripped himself with his broom, trying to keep the chair from banging to the floor. "Got to get her cleaned up, mister. You'd be surprised how early some folks start coming in."

"I don't know why they even bothered to go home," Hale growled. He strapped his gun belt on and went outside. In the pale light the town was a miserable-looking place — shacks and tents and piles of gravel. He saw ice along the edges of the creek and on water-splashed boulders in the stream.

He looked up toward Terrible Pass. It was enough to turn an empty stomach. He saw the faint outline of a trail that looked like a feeble scratch across the face of cold rock.

Snow was hanging in the V-troughs. The massive mountain seemed to be just waiting there in the half-light for some damned fool to try to climb it.

By nine o'clock he was outfitted and ready to go. The prices were not only higher than in Denver, they were higher than anywhere else in the whole world. He had not made a very good deal in his trade for mules with Clint Aiken, who undoubtedly was making up his losses on the wheel of fortune the night before.

"You'll have to watch old Molly there," Aiken said, indicating the brown pack mule. "Give her half a chance and she'll head for home like a turpentined dog going through a cabbage patch." He looked up the mountain. "I don't even know why you want to go over there. Late last fall we heard some wild tales about a strike at Spanish Creek, but I think it was all hot air. Now if you're looking for a claim. . . ."

"Who built that trail?" Hale asked.

"Indians, Spanish, mountain men . . . nobody rightly knows. Prospectors fixed it up a little. It ain't much of a trail."

Hale got on his riding mule.

"If Aaron Bliffert is still over there, tell him hello for me," Aiken said.

"Do you know him well?"

"Business dealings. Him and some of the boys used to come over now and then to have a time. He's some fellow, old Aaron. When he's around, you laugh your head off."

Or get it blown off, Hale thought. He rode away.

Before he had gone a quarter of a mile, he knew that Blaine had made no mistake in insisting that he use mules. The trail was steep, one zigzag after another. Winter-loosened rocks and dirt made it slant sharply to the outside. The seams of the mountain were full of snow and ice. Sure-footed, nimble, the mules picked their way where Hale would have hesitated to put a horse. Instead of lunging into the discolored snow, they eased into it and felt their way through.

Mindful of what Aiken had said of Molly, Hale had her ahead of him. She went along sweetly, but Hale was not deceived by that. A mule was a mule, he knew. One of his father's wise old stable hands had once told him: "For thirty years some mules is nothing but pure faithful, just waiting for that one chance to get you in the belly with both hind feet."

Resting just before a switchback, Hale looked down at Silver Bell. He was startled to see how much altitude he had gained. But he was not startled to see Louis just starting up the trail with his two mules. *You've got your business and I've got mine.* Louis had damned well better keep it that way.

After the initial quick rise, the trail became less steep. It curled around the rocky buttresses of the mountain and went through timber where the snow was deeper than any Hale had encountered previously. Old Molly was still a willing leader, breaking the crusted barrier, resting as she pleased.

Hale got off and led his mule. He had bought high boots and a heavy sheepskin coat in Silver Bell, and he was thankful for them now as he fought the snow. Under the crust it was a shifting mass of coarse crystals. Old Molly's shod hoofs cut clear through to the rock surface, but Hale's lesser weight left him floundering. Thigh deep, the snow made a dry, swishing sound against his legs. It shifted readily, but never offered stable footing.

He was glad to break out of the timber and see the trail ahead in a long slant along a dry slope. Far above was a gap between two great shoulders of the mountain. If that was the summit, things were going very well. The sun was warm, there was only a slight wind, and a cloudless sky promised a fair day.

Hale was looking down at the tiny rectangles that were the tents and cabins of Silver Bell when old Molly made her move. The trail was narrow. There was no room for her to turn, let alone get past Hale. Without warning or any hesitation she went over the edge of the trail, partly sliding and leaping to reach a rock-strewn ledge. She turned back there, weaving through the broken granite, back past Hale, who had just remounted. He swung down as quickly as he could and tried to intercept her as she came up to the trail. Her long neck stretched out, her hoofs digging. Molly made it just ahead of him. She gained the trail and headed back for Silver Bell, into the timber, her hoofs kicking snow. Hale saw her come out on the other side and go around a point of rocks, taking her time now. All that lung-busting altitude lost in minutes.

The riding mule would not leave the trail where Molly had gone. Hale had to go 200 yards before he found a place to turn the animal. If old Molly's pack slipped, or if she tried to rub it off against some of those rocky walls, she would be in big trouble.

It was unlikely, though, that either would happen. The mule would go all the way back to Silver Bell, and then Hale would be hailed there as not only the man who slept with niggers, but as the flatlander who had lost his whole outfit on a simple trip up a mountain. Yes, sir, Ezekiel Blaine had picked a good man for his big deal at Spanish Creek. A careless, five-thumbed ape, that's what. At the moment, Hale had a burning wish that he could tell Aiken what to do with his mule, and Blaine what he could do with his gold express.

Knowing that she was headed for the home corral, Hale's mule went down the mountain briskly. Fifteen minutes later, Hale met Molly head-on at a sharp turn in the trail. Behind her was Louis with his two mules.

"What are you doing here?" Hale yelled.

Louis grinned. "Gathering stray animals and things."

"You're following me, you grinning black hellion!"

"Black, I am, but I'm not following you, and I haven't lost either of my mules."

Under the circumstances there was nothing Hale could win from Louis, and Hale knew it. He took the wise course. He held his temper. Getting his mule turned was a tricky, tight chore. At one point in the maneuver he almost got brushed off the trail.

"Sure is a long way down there," Louis observed. "Might bruise a man a little."

Hale put a rope on old Molly. The next time she tried to break away, she would have to take the other mule with her. Mounted and ready to go, Hale yelled back to Louis: "You waited to let me break trail, eh?"

"I hung back just to catch runaway mules. For no thanks, too." Louis sounded like his temper had worn a little thin.

He fell behind as they went on up toward the pass. Before he again reached the place where Molly had made her break, Hale observed that the weather was changing fast. The sky was clouded, the wind was stronger, colder. He went on without incident to the notch in the gray planes of harsh granite.

From there he got the full impact of what lay ahead. He had reached a crest, sure enough, but it was only the beginning. Far beyond the sparse and scraggly timber where he was, the snow-splotched trail went up and up, above the last of the timber, on up through rough slide rock and on to where it undoubtedly had to pass between two mighty wedges of a mountain that he had not even seen from Silver Bell.

For a mile the riding was easy. Cairns of gray stones marked the way across a grassy swale. Some of them barely protruded above banks of snow that caused Hale to make long detours. He looked back and saw Louis a quarter of a mile behind him.

Lifting up from the grassy swale, Hale began to encounter snowdrifts that he could not go around. His mount broke through the first two in strong surges, but balked at the third one. The yellowish-crusted barrier blocked the trail completely, a cliff on one side, an overhang of rock on the other.

Hale got down and wallowed through it, up to his waist. Returning, he saw Molly rearing back against her towline, trying to drag the other mule around. He ran back and swung his weight hard on the rope, and the pack mule steadied down.

Louis was just coming up from the grassy place.

Borne by an increasing wind, the storm came in while Hale was leading his mules through the drift. The sudden, almost blinding fury of the tempest reminded Hale of storms he had seen on the plains. In minutes the sullen air was thick with the big, spinning flakes and he could see only a short distance ahead. One side of the mules was wet with melting snow. He was breaking through another drift on foot, hanging hard to the reins of his mule, when he heard Louis come up with his animals. Hale's mule almost ran over him with its last surge on the far side of the drift.

Then, for a few hundred yards, the trail was clear, except that the snow was beginning to stick to it. Aiken had said that the higher one went on Terrible Pass, the less snow he was likely to encounter because winds scoured the high reaches of the mountains with terrible force during the winter. In the whirling blizzard Hale no longer could estimate how high he was. He could not see the swale he had crossed or the heights where he had yet to go.

The next drift he struck was impossible. As he tried to force his way through it, he fell in up to his armpits. Backing out, he fell against the legs of the mule and for a moment was fearful of being trampled, but the animal rocked back in alarm, its shoes clanging on the cold rock. With snow melting on his face and his wet clothes seeping cold against his legs, Hale scrambled up. He studied the snowdrift. He was feeling the altitude. With a hellish expenditure of energy he could break through the drift, but how many more were ahead, and how far was it to that gunsight notch he could no longer see?

Louis worked his way up beside the mules. His face was gleaming with wetness. He looked at the drift and merely stood there, offering nothing. It further irritated Hale to note that Louis was wearing heavy woolen mittens and a warm scarf. No Negro should look so calm and warm and secure in the midst of a raging storm that dislocated a man from the wild mountain and everything else a hundred feet away. Louis said nothing.

After a time Hale cursed and said: "Well?"

"You want help?"

Hale could not ask for it. "We're not on the same trail!"

"If you want help, you ask for it. You're a long way from the mansion house now, Brother Hale."

"One of these times I'm going to. . . ." Hale did not finish the threat. It was no more use in the situation than if shouted at the snowy rocks. And Louis waited. "We need each other's help," Hale said.

"I guess that's about as close as a Southern gentleman like you could come to it." Louis walked into the snowdrift.

V

Where they had no choice because of cliffs, they smashed through the drifts on foot. In other places Louis decided whether they could go around or not. Hale's hands were torn and streaked with frozen blood from moving stones at the by-passes. Some of the places Louis picked looked impassable, but after he led the first mule across, the others followed. In three hours of struggle they reached what Hale thought was the pass. The wind was funneling through the gap, driving snow crystals with biting force. One side of the mules was plastered white, and icicles hung from their muzzles.

Now there was an openness around them that puzzled Hale. He had expected more cliffs and a narrow trail, but they were moving across an almost level place. Stumbling along, benumbed by cold and altitude, he no longer tried to guess what lay around them. Louis was in the lead. It was he who kept direction by the lonely cairns that stood beside the trail, one side of them white from the sweep of the storm. Ice was forming on the rocks. The mules minced along carefully.

They started up a steep grade, and Hale could see that they were back in barren granite again. The pass was a slot that broke a mighty ridge. They went through it and started down.

"Got to get to timber," Louis said.

They came to the first low-growing shrubs, bent to the east by the eternal force of the wind, and then to scraggly trees with branches on only one side, and then the dark green firs appeared, and they reached a hollow in the mountain where the wind seemed to be suddenly shut off. The snow was still falling.

Louis took care of the mules while Hale was building a fire with fingers that felt like wooden sticks. Beside a tangled windfall the flames became their proof of victory.

Hale warmed beside it, watching Louis giving oats to the mules. Louis fed them all impartially. "I couldn't get any oats in Silver Bell," Hale said. "I'll pay you for my share."

"Never mind. The mules don't care who pays or not."

"All right. I won't then," Hale said curtly.

They cooked on the same fire, each preparing his own meal. Louis fried potatoes and onions in one pan and great slabs of bacon in another. Hale wanted to ask where he had gotten the potatoes, but he did not inquire. They ate without talking to each other.

Afterward Hale knocked more limbs from

the windfall and built up the fire. While snowflakes hissed softly in the flames, he lit a cigar and refilled his tin cup with coffee. Now that they were safe, Louis's competence on the mountain was a memory that irked Hale.

"Louis, what's your business in Spanish Creek?"

"I didn't ask you that question, Brother Hale."

"I'm not your brother!"

"You didn't say that when we were over there in those snowdrifts. You standing there like an old woman and too proud to say . . . 'Louis, I need your help. You're a dirty black bastard, but I need your help.' "

Hale tried to hold his temper. "I don't have to dislike you because you're black, and that isn't reason enough for me to like you, either, but, by God, I'm getting so I can't stand the sight of you."

"The feeling is mutual, Brother Hale."

Hale threw his cup down, but he forgot the cigar. He lunged forward to punch Louis in the jaw. Louis ducked far enough so that the blow took him in the forehead. It knocked him back, but not down. Hale expected him to come springing in like a big cat. He intended to take Louis low and let the man's own surge help throw him over

Hale's back and into the windfall beyond.

Louis came shuffling instead. Hale missed him with a hard swing. Louis's first blow shattered Hale's cigar and drove fire into his cheek bone. The next one, quick following, was a rib rattler that made Hale gasp. He grabbed Louis and hung on, forcing him back to keep him from getting solid footing for a blow.

They both fell into the snow-covered rocks away from the fire. For an instant Hale thought he had him. He got his wrist across Louis's throat and tried to drive it down with the heel of his right hand. The man was a convulsive, powerful bundle of muscle. He exploded upward and rolled Hale to one side. Before Hale could recover, Louis was on top of him and had him by the throat. As best he could from his prone position, Hale hammered Louis in the side of the neck. The blows seemed to have no effect.

Suddenly the weight was gone from Hale and he could breathe again. Louis had let go and leaped away. As Hale scrambled to his feet, he saw the reason. In their struggle they had rolled in close to the mules and frightened them. Molly had broken her halter rope and was swinging around, headed uphill. Louis got the end of the rope in a desperate dive that put him flat on his belly. The mule dragged him a short distance before she slowed, and then Louis snubbed the rope around a tree.

The other three mules were plunging, straining at their halter ropes. For a few moments disaster threatened. Hale went in close, talking to the animals. He stretched his arms wide to grab two halters, and for a time he was off the ground as the mules reared back. Louis, having tied Molly, came back to calm the third animal.

The mules secure again, their tie ropes and halter buckles checked, Hale and Louis went back to the fire. Their blood lust had been stilled by the incident, but they were both sullenly alert as they brushed snow from their clothing and eyed each other.

After a time Louis said: "I got a bad mouth."

"I have a careless temper."

They let it go at that.

A little later Louis looked at his watch. He knew about Hale's useless timepiece, so he turned his own so Hale could read it. Six o'clock. The storm had made it seem much later. There was not a mark on Louis that Hale could see. His own ribs were aching, his right hand was swollen, and the cigar burn on his cheek was hurting.

Louis took the first two hours of guard duty that night. After he got into his blankets under a cold-crackling rubber poncho, Hale slipped his right hand out into the snow to ease the ache. He dozed off, and, when he pulled his hand under the blankets later, it felt as if it had frozen.

Louis roused him at four hours, instead of two, giving him the watch. "Your Molly mule keeps trying to untie that knot."

"I'll watch her."

The snow had stopped. Hale built up the fire. He tried heat treatment on his swollen hand, but found it less effective as a pain-killer than cold. At intervals he heard Molly's gnawing at her rope. Each time he walked toward her, she stopped and appeared to be dozing. He made a mental note to unload her on some Yankee horse trader the very moment he no longer needed her. That would be after he got to Spanish Creek and back to Denver with more than 100 pounds of gold dust and nuggets.

He let Louis sleep his full hours. It was so close to daylight then that Hale started breakfast. While he was cooking, Louis packed his mules and prepared to leave. "I'll break trail on this side."

It was an hour later before Hale left. Although he was descending a south slope,

171

there was deep snow in the timber. He could see that Louis had worked hard to break trail. To come back by the same route would be slow, exhausting toil.

Hale got his first view of Spanish Creek from 2,000 feet above the valley. He saw smoke drifting above the brown of willows and dead grass. Tiny figures moved beside a looping stream. Although it had stormed furiously on the mountain the night before, there was no snow in the valley.

The sun came out and glittered on the stream far below. The reflection on the snow where Hale was made him clamp his eyes down to watery slits. After he broke out of the snow, the descent was easy, the last of it winding down a slope through leafless aspens. He saw a low, dirt-roofed cabin ahead. A lank, bearded man was watching him from the doorway. When he was still some distance from the cabin, he saw a second man sitting in the warm sun on a rock beside the trail. *Watch every word you say from now on,* Hale told himself.

The man rose and waved his hand in a rough salute. "Welcome to Spanish Creek, Brother Hale!" White teeth flashed in a golden beard. The man's face was round, with long wrinkles in the forehead. His eyes were bright blue. Good humor was the mark of him.

"You know me?" Hale asked.

"I do now. The nigra, Louis, said there was a preaching man named Brother Hale coming down behind him, but I'd say you don't look much like no preacher." The man's accent was strongly Southern.

"I'm no preacher," Hale said. He dismounted.

"Ewan Fitzpatrick. Ragged Fitzpatrick, as the winter goes, and also Thirsty Fitzpatrick." They shook hands, and then Fitzpatrick held up two fingers. "One, how many gallons of whiskey do you have in that pack? Two, do you have a sound deck of the devil's instruments?"

Hale grinned. "I've got one quart of whiskey. No playing cards."

"Ten dollars for the quart!"

"You can have it for showing me a claim where I can make a million."

"The easiest bargain I ever made," Fitzpatrick said. They went on down to the cabin, and he would not be satisfied until Hale had slipped the pack and produced the whiskey. The man who had been standing in the doorway came forward and watched the proceedings with a sour expression.

173

"Bob Giles," Fitzpatrick said. "He's got a bad belly and can't drink a drop, praise heaven."

Giles nodded gloomily. He was a tall man with a ragged black beard and dark, burning eyes. Hale observed that he studied everything in the opened pack. "Have you got any newspapers in them panniers?" he asked.

"No, I haven't."

"Nothing at all to read?"

"No."

"Christ!" Giles turned away and went into the cabin.

"He got a Minié ball in the guts at the stone wall with Kershaw at Fredericksburg," Fitzpatrick said. "I was with Cobb myself." He took his second long pull from the bottle and passed it on to Hale. "How about you?"

"Pickett. Kemper's brigade." Hale knew he was among Southerners, sure enough, but where was Steve Munson? He decided to move with caution until he had a grasp of affairs in Spanish Creek. No telling what changes had taken place during the long winter.

Making gurgling inroads on the bottle, Fitzpatrick went with him to the creek. Hale staked the mules out in the grass.

"What happened to your hand there?"

Fitzpatrick asked.

"Sprained it."

"And did you sprain your cheek, too?"

"Hit a low limb."

"Did it happen to have a big black fist on the end of it?" Fitzpatrick laughed. "And when you straighten up, you show a bit of tenderness in the ribs."

Hale revised his estimate of Fitzpatrick; the man was plenty shrewd. Louis would not have said anything about that senseless brawl up there on the mountain, Hale was sure.

"What's Louis's business here?" Fitzpatrick asked.

"The same as mine, as far as I know. He came to dig a pot full of gold."

"I hope so." Fitzpatrick's bright blue eyes were merry. He held out the bottle toward Hale, who took it with his left hand. "That right paw is pretty sore, eh? You must have hit him on top of the head."

Far up the creek, Hale saw the smoke above the willows. "Everyone's at work, huh?"

"Our boys are all out hunting. They'll be back, but not before we finish off the whiskey. Now you're real sure you haven't got another one?"

"That's it."

"But you would have a bite or two of something to eat in the panniers? We've been living on elk and them rabbits with the big feet for three long months."

"I think I can find something."

They both had to duck to go through the doorway of the cabin. It was much bigger inside than Hale had thought, since almost half of it was dug into the hill. The odor of it struck him like the rank den of animals — old sweat and filthy blankets and all the sickening smells that only man can create.

Coming out of bright sunlight, he had trouble making out details in the gloomy place while his eyes were expanding to the dimness. There was a fireplace in the dugout end, the fire itself down to coals. That and a tiny window covered with hide gave the only illumination after Fitzpatrick pulled the slab door shut. Down the middle of the room was a long table of hewed poles. Along the walls there were pole bunks for at least twenty-five men, Hale estimated. Among the items of food he put down on the table was a lard bucket of eggs, each one wrapped in crumpled newspaper.

A man coughed and groaned weakly in one of the bunks. Peering toward the sound, Hale made out a lumped figure and a pale brow. He thought it must be Giles, but a

176

moment later Giles heaved out of another bunk and came over to the table.

"Canned tomatoes. By God!" He pried the lid off the lard bucket. "Eggs!" He began to take the crumpled paper off them. "And something to read, too!"

Hale glanced at Fitzpatrick, who had the bottle tilted again. "It must have been a long, hard winter."

"Depends on how you look at it." Fitzpatrick wiped his mouth. "I thought we got along pretty good." He shrugged. "A few like Walt there had hard luck." He motioned toward the man in the bunk. "Chopped his foot with an axe, and then he got pneumonia." He shook his head. "Poor old Walt. Fix him a couple of those eggs, Giles. They might make him perk up a little."

"Fix them yourself," Giles grumbled. "I do enough cooking around here as it is."

For an instant Fitzpatrick's eyes were like two chips of blue ice, but he laughed and said: "You wouldn't want Major Hale to think that I'm not the first sergeant in this den, would you? *Please* cook the food, Mister Giles." He winked at Hale.

"None of your damned Irish soft soap!" Giles said. He meant it; the words were vicious. He prepared the food without further complaint, cooking on the coals of the fireplace. When it came time to cut the loaf of bread Hale had supplied, Giles drew a wicked-looking knife from his belt. Dried blood and animal hair were matted at the hilt. The edge was gray and razor-keen.

All the while the man in the bunk kept coughing.

The cold-storage eggs had an ancient, musty taste, but Giles and Fitzpatrick wolfed them and everything else down without a pause. Then Fitzpatrick said: "Damn! We didn't save a couple for Walt."

"He's about done," Giles grunted.

"Poor old Walt," Fitzpatrick sighed, and raised the bottle.

"A friend of Aaron Bliffert's wanted me to say hello for him," Hale said. "Where do I find Bliffert?"

Giles was wiping out the frying pan with a piece of bread. For an instant he was dead still, the piece of bread poised above the congealing grease. From the corner of his eye, Hale saw Fitzpatrick staring at him with a cold expression. All of it was over in a second or two. Then Giles shoved the bread into his mouth, and Fitzpatrick gestured toward the creek with the bottle. "Poor old Aaron."

"He's sick, too?"

"Dead these five days," Fitzpatrick said

178

sadly. "And here's to his memory." He drank. "Ah, Aaron. . . . He was a man to make you laugh fit to kill. Who was the friend who asked about him?"

"The livery man in Silver Bell."

"A thief, that one. I bought a horse from him. And here's to his downfall." Fitzpatrick tipped the bottle.

It was, Hale observed, about two-thirds gone. Fitzpatrick should have been bleary-eyed drunk, but, aside from a flush above the golden beard, he showed no sign of having had a drop. He rose suddenly and stepped back over the bench. "On to fame and riches, bucko! I'll now show you where you can pick up nuggets by the bucketful."

"He can have one of the claims close by," Giles suggested. "That way he could stay with us."

There was something other than hospitality in that offer, Hale was sure.

"I'll decide on the claim," Fitzpatrick said. "You've never mined before, Major?"

"Never a lick."

"And . . . ah . . . Louis?"

"I don't know. The tools on his pack mule looked used, but maybe he bought them that way in Denver."

Fitzpatrick opened the door. Hale was going toward it, and now the sudden light blinded him. "You came all the way from Denver with him?" Fitzpatrick asked.

The questions were irking Hale, but he controlled himself carefully. "I ran into him in Silver Bell, night before last."

"You didn't know him?" Giles asked.

"I'd seen him around Denver, yes." The choking cough of the sick man followed Hale into the sunlight. The air had a good clean smell. It was the real world out here; he hoped he would never have to go into the den again.

Fitzpatrick led him upstream past piles of yellow gravel near the creek and test holes that had been dug among the willows farther from the river. The holes were nearly full of water. Fitzpatrick waved the bottle like a pointer. "We gouged around all through here. No good."

"Doesn't it take a bigger stream than this for gold?"

Fitzpatrick laughed. "It's where you find it, Major. It was *major,* wasn't it?"

"Captain."

"That Louis fellow never spoke of mining all the time you were together?"

Damn the quick-shifting questions, Hale thought. He had plenty of his own, although he could not ask them. "We didn't talk much," he said. "We weren't together all the time on the pass."

"You talked enough to fight. What caused that?"

Hale ignored the question. "I thought you were going to show me some ground I can work."

Fitzpatrick grinned. "I'll drink to that."

They came to where four men were working at a sluice box of whipsawed lumber. The miners stopped and gathered around a fire on a gravel bar — bearded young men in ragged, filthy clothing and broken boots.

"The big rush is on," Fitzpatrick said, "and Hale here is the first one." He gave the bottle to a square-jawed man whose shaggy brown hair was sticking through rents in an old felt hat. "Ed Allen, Hale. Union gunner, but he's trying to reform."

"Hell I am," Allen said. He shook hands with Hale. "You're not the first. A Negro just went up the creek an hour or so ago."

"He don't count," Fitzpatrick said. He looked at the riffles in the sluice. "Getting rich as usual, eh?"

"Oh, sure!" Allen said. He was civil, but not friendly, and that was the way Hale read the whole group. Allen had not taken a drink, but he had passed the bottle on. His companions were certainly not abstainers.

"Hey, there! Watch it, boys!" Fitzpatrick

spoke too late. One of the miners was drinking the last of the whiskey. Fitzpatrick rolled his eyes to the sky. "A fine bunch of drunkards, I must say. Come on, Hale, let's get away from these sots."

They passed another group at a sluice. Fitzpatrick hailed some of them by name, but he did not stop to visit.

Hale was hard put to keep from asking questions. So far he had not heard one name that he recognized from his talk with Ezekiel Blaine. Aaron Bliffert, yes, but he was dead.

They struck an area where the creek was broken into several small streams that wandered among the willows. Fitzpatrick skipped across each branch like a playful boy. "How'd you hear about Spanish Creek, Hale?"

"There was a drunk throwing money around the saloon like a Yankee cavalryman."

"Denver?"

"Yes."

"Allen's bunch have got their huts across the creek in the timber. You couldn't see them from where we were unless you knew. Did you talk to this drunk?"

"I didn't have to. You could hear him all over town. He said he'd just come from here, and the way he was spending gold on faro bank. . . ."

"Lowe. We all worried about that boy. He went out of here in a fierce storm one night. Bless him for making it through. What saloon did you talk to him in?"

"The Big Nugget is where I heard him. . . . Fitzpatrick, I've had enough of your questions."

Fitzpatrick laughed. "Excuse me, Major."

They left the branching streams and went along the edge of the aspens where travel was easier, and then they came to where the creek was one flow again.

Louis's mules were picketed in the winter-bent grass. On a level place at the edge of the aspens he had erected a lean-to shelter. He was building a fire when Hale and Fitzpatrick walked in on him. Louis nodded in answer to Fitzpatrick's greeting, but to Hale he gave only a sullen look.

For ten minutes Fitzpatrick talked about the regulations of the mining district. Sometimes in the middle of a sentence he hit Louis with quick, shrewd questions that had nothing to do with mining. All of Louis's answers bore out the information Fitzpatrick had gotten from Hale.

"The Spanish Creek district runs two miles along the creek," Fitzpatrick said.

"Right here you're about a half mile from the eastern end. Everything up that way is open ground. You can stake one claim, a hundred feet wide and two hundred feet long. As long as you keep working it, it's yours. You can buy as many claims as you want from someone else, but one claim is all you can stake. After you mark it out, it costs one dollar to record it."

"Where do you do that?" Hale asked.

"Giles is the district recorder. Give him a description of the ground and one dollar. That's all you have to do."

"This is all legal?" Hale asked. "We own the ground we stake?"

"As long as you keep working it."

"Every day, you mean?" Louis asked.

"You can go hunting or be sick or something like that for a few days, but you can't just hold onto the ground and do nothing with it. If anything like that comes up, you ask me. I'm the sheriff." Fitzpatrick grinned. "And the judge."

"Both, huh?" Hale said.

"Duly elected."

Hale looked at the creek. "There's lots of gold in that gravel, eh?"

"There's just one way to find out," Fitzpatrick said. He walked away, breaking into song after a few steps.

Louis stooped over, moving stones at his fire site. "They've already got a man over there in the trees to the south, watching us."

"Who's *they?*"

"You know more about that than I do."

Hale turned away. He went down the valley about 100 yards and found a place that looked like a good campsite. He cleared the dead aspens away, putting them in a pile for firewood. He did not take much time at the task because he was worried about his pack.

Going back toward the den — it was a fitting name — he appraised his knowledge so far of the situation in Spanish Creek and concluded that he was woefully ignorant of what was going on. He retraced the same trail he and Fitzpatrick had used, passing the miners on the creek. They seemed even less friendly now than they had been when he was with Fitzpatrick, although Allen paused long enough in his shoveling to ask if he had decided on ground to stake.

When Hale answered, Allen nodded and said: "It's as likely a place as any, I suppose."

A half dozen men who Hale had not seen before were at the den. Some of them were cutting up parts of an elk on a stump. Giles seemed to be directing the operation.

Someone had gone through Hale's pan-

185

niers. He could tell that by the lumps of careless repacking. Fitzpatrick came up to him while Hale was hefting the canvas sacks. "Is rifling a man's packs against one of your regulations in this district?" Hale asked angrily.

Fitzpatrick's face was a study in outrage. "God damn you, Giles!" he roared, and plunged away toward the stump where they were cutting up the elk meat.

Giles had a knife in his hand, but Fitzpatrick drove him back into the cabin by curses and shouts, and followed him out a short time later, with Giles carrying a sack of canned goods. Giles's expression was murderous as he dumped the cans beside the panniers and walked away.

"Once a thief, always a thief," Fitzpatrick growled. "That son-of-a-bitch even took the aces from the one deck of cards we got left. Is that everything?"

"Good enough," Hale said.

Fitzpatrick helped him load the pack mule. "You're sure you haven't got just maybe a pint somewhere?"

"You could have it if I had one."

Fitzpatrick sighed. "I've a mind to send a man to Silver Bell, but it snowed on the pass last night."

"It did that. I was in it."

"Where was Lowe, you say, when you heard him blowing his mouth off?"

It almost trapped Hale. He was looking down at a rope when the question struck and that gave him time to think before he met Fitzpatrick's eyes on the other side of Molly. Hale gave the knot a tug, shaking his swollen hand afterward. "I heard him in the Big Nugget. What are you after, Fitzpatrick?"

"Nothing at all, Major. I have a bad memory."

They finished packing the mule, and Hale mounted the other one. "I'll be camped just this side of where the nigger is. If you have any spare time, I'd sure be thankful for any advice you care to give me about mining."

"I'll do that."

Hale was riding away when one of the men at the stump cried: "Munson, damn your hide! You're cutting that meat cross-grained!"

The name hit home, and for the second time in minutes Hale was almost trapped, but he had been honed to a fine alertness ever since he'd arrived. He barely managed not to jerk his head around to look at the man called Munson.

Where the trail led through the mass of wandering streams to avoid a jutting hill,

Hale chose to take his mules to more solid ground north of the river. It was then he crossed a little stream he had not seen before. It came down in small cascades from a dense thicket of fir trees, and beside it was a well-defined trail. He tried to see what lay up that way, but the trees stood too closely together.

He went on and made his camp. The sun was gone by the time he was set up. Chill from the abundant moisture of the valley was being carried by a light evening breeze. Carrying out his rôle as an eager gold-seeker, Hale went down to the creek to make a claim. He floundered through the willows that overhung the banks of the stream until he came to a gravel bar that looked like an easier place to dig than anywhere among the tough-rooted willows. He was then upstream from Louis's camp, and he could see Louis lounging by his fire with a cup of coffee.

Hale paced off the distances and staked his claim. South across the river stood a tall dead spruce tree in the water of a small beaver pond. That would do for a reference mark and an excuse to go across it and see if he could spot the man that Louis had said was spying on them. He made a show of pacing off the distance to the tree, at the same time studying the timber beyond it.

He saw no sign of any watcher, but, while he was standing there writing down the distance, he heard a twig crack somewhere back in the thicket.

As he approached Louis's camp on his way back to his own campsite, he observed how comfortably Louis was set up, a warm fire reflecting heat back into the lean-to shelter, cooking utensils hanging on a crossbar between two trees — a simple neatness about the whole place. Louis had cut aspen poles and lashed them together to make a chair.

Hale wanted to stop and visit. In fact, he wished he could camp with Louis. They were both under heavy suspicion in Spanish Creek. They had been purposely thrown close together so they could be watched. That made them outcasts and allies because they had a common enemy.

As Hale passed the camp, glancing casually at the man in the chair, Louis murmured: "He was there. He moved back when you started toward that tree."

Hale gave a tiny nod and walked on.

Ezekiel Blaine had spoken somewhat vaguely of using decoys to confuse Bliffert's bunch, but he had brushed away Hale's efforts to find out more about the plan. Now

Hale wondered if Louis was one of the decoys. Whatever he was, caution dictated that they must continue the pretense of having no use for each other.

Beside the fire in his own camp, Hale watched darkness sliding down the mountains to the south. Blaine certainly had been right about Spanish Creek's being a remote and isolated place. To the east and to the west, those tremendous mountains with snow fields that looked bluish in the fading light appeared to be impassable. But Hale knew there was a low pass to the east that led to the wide grasslands of Big Bayou. Blaine had told him that he would have to use his own judgment about the route to use when it came time to make his run with the gold.

Before Hale went to bed, he brought Molly up from the creek and tied her, close to the camp. He slept only lightly that night, aware of every sound.

No one came near the camp. But in the middle of the night the riding mule pulled loose its picket pin and came up to join Molly. A mule could feel as lonely as a human being, Hale knew.

VI

For five days Hale worked harder than he ever had in all his life. He had never made any bones about it to himself or anyone else — he hated manual labor. He shoveled tons of wet and slippery rocks to get down to the sand that lay below them, and then he squatted until his knees and legs were numb, panning the sand.

Fitzpatrick came up several times to teach him how to pan. Hale got the hang of it, all right, but it seemed like a sorry way to try for riches. Put some gravel and sand in, dip water, slosh the damned thing at a tilt and spill the lighter contents over the edge of the pan, and keep that up until you were down to the last black sand. And that was where the streak of dull yellow was supposed to show up. Hale got flecks, instead of streaks.

"Flash in the pan," Fitzpatrick said, hugely amused. "You've got to do better than that, Major."

"How?"

"Well, you dig in a different place on your claim until you find rich gravel, and then you build a sluice."

Hale's feet were wet and cold. He cast a bleak look at the piles of gravel he had already moved. If he got away from the open bar where he had chosen to work, he would have to uproot willows and sod. "I've had more fun than this fighting Indians."

"There's no money in that. How's the nigra doing?"

Hale glanced up the creek where Louis was working. "I don't know, but I'm going to find out, and I'm also going around and watch some of the others. What's the penalty for stealing gold in this district?"

Fitzpatrick laughed. "A hundred lashes. It's never come up."

"What did Giles get for stealing my grub?"

"Twenty lashes, but I suspended sentence because of the terrible condition of his belly and the fact that he's always been a thief. Did you ever hear of a man named Ezekiel Blaine?"

Hale thought a moment. "Yeah. The man with the crippled arm. He runs a saloon in Denver."

The bright blue eyes were hard on Hale. "Crippled arm, you say?"

"He carries it in a sling. I supposed it was crippled or something."

As was his habit, Fitzpatrick seemed to forget the subject instantly. "Try another part of your ground. You don't have to stay in the creek. You might find a rich pocket right or left, or even hanging on a tree." He went on top to visit Louis.

Hale went out into the willows and began to dig a test hole, starting where an old beaver run offered easier excavation than among the willow roots. It was not long before he gave up and wandered down the creek to visit Ed Allen and his group. His reception there was not cordial. In all, there were ten men. Although they had three sluice boxes, the entire group was now working only one. Allen came the closest to being friendly, but, at that, he was no more than civil. He answered Hale's questions about sluice work, but volunteered no other information.

The divisions and conflicts on Spanish Creek were still unclear to Hale. It certainly was not the simple thing that Blaine had described. Allen's group was probably in-betweeners. That was a sorry row of cotton to hoe, if conditions were as Blaine had said, but it was the way of some men to try to stand aside from both right and wrong. To be nothing.

Hale went on down the stream. The den had to be enemy, but that was confusion, too. If there really was a man named Munson in that group, then things were rather badly mixed. Fitzpatrick and Giles were Southerners, probably Georgians, but the way Blaine had put it, Bliffert's gang was Northern white trash. And just what had happened to Bliffert?

Strong in Hale's mind was the little branch stream that ran up into the fir trees. The trail was there, but he had seen no marks of recent usage in it. Blaine had said that the Southerners, original locators of the placer camp, had been shoved away from their first claims and had struck it rich on a tributary creek.

On the stream above and below the den, Hale saw six sluice boxes. Only a few men were at work. At the den men were sitting on stumps or lying around in the sunny yard like big birds outside an unclean roost. He had seen plenty of rags and tatters during the war, and young faces hardened from constant living with death and privation, but there was a quality of animal-like wariness and viciousness in the men before him now that set them aside from any group of soldiers he had known. Not one of them spoke or gave him any sign of greeting as he walked past them and went into the den. It was his third visit inside. The second one had been when he filed his claim with Giles, who had taken the dollar and tossed the description on the table.

The place had not improved itself. Hale

called out in the gloom, and Giles got out of a bunk and came over to the table. "What do you want now?"

"I want to turn my claim back, so I can find a better one."

"All you soft-handed nabobs are the same," Giles sneered. "A few hours' work and you ain't got rich, so. . . ."

"I don't need your guff, Giles. All I want is another claim."

"You can abandon it, or you can sell it, but, either way, you can't stake another claim."

"Why not? Fitzpatrick said. . . ."

"Fitzpatrick, Fitzpatrick! He's always mouthing off." Giles raked his fingers through his stringy hair. "All right, I'll buy your claim, and we'll stretch the rules a little, and you can stake another one. One dollar."

"You mean that's what you'll give me?"

"I just said it, didn't I?"

"That isn't much, Giles."

"Forget it then." Giles turned away.

"I'll take it."

"It's two dollars recording fee when you switch claims, so give me a dollar."

"I haven't staked my new one yet."

"Pay it now and you won't be back here bothering me. Fitzpatrick can tell me where it is, and I'll make a record of it."

Hale put the dollar on the table. It slipped between the hewed poles and fell on the dirt floor. Stooping to pick it up, he saw in a shaft of sunlight from the open door the description he had filed before. He retrieved it and threw it on the table with the dollar. "Is that how you record claims in this district?"

"Hell, it don't matter, since you said it was no good anyway." Giles picked up the dollar.

With the idea of getting as close as possible to where he thought the Southerners to be, Hale was staking a new claim on the branch creek an hour later. In the cool gloom of the thicket he neither heard nor saw the man until a harsh voice said: "Hold it steady right there!"

The man was still indistinct, but the rifle was not. "Unbuckle that gun belt."

Hale obeyed.

"Now your knife."

"All I have is a pocket knife. I think. . . ."

"Put it on the ground."

Again Hale obeyed. "Who are you?"

The man stepped from the trees. He was tall and thin, and the whites of his eyes looked enormous in the gloom, and his face was gaunt, as if from illness. "Now we'll march down the trail, and, if you want to make a break for it, try it."

He was a Southerner, Hale realized. "Wait a minute. I think you and I can. . . ."

The man cracked the rifle. "March, god damn you!"

When they came out on the jutting hill and turned downstream, everyone on the creek could see them. Allen's men stayed where they were, but Louis left his work to follow Hale and his captor.

The man took Hale straight to the den. Grinning men rose from their loafing, laughing, gibing. "Would you look at that!" one cried. "Old Munson has done caught hisself a Southern rooster!"

Fitzpatrick was sitting on a stump, watching with an amused expression.

"All right, Fitzpatrick," Munson said. "You make the big noise about laws in this district. I caught this man trying to jump Fatty Mitchell's claim. What are you going to do about it?"

"Is that so, Hale?" Fitzpatrick rose and put one foot on the stump.

"I didn't know it was staked ground," Hale said. "If I had known. . . ."

"If the dog hadn't stopped to crap, he would have caught the rabbit," someone said, and the men laughed.

"All right, let's have some order!" Fitzpatrick roared. He pointed to a slight, sharp-faced youth. "Peters."

The youth ran into the cabin and returned with an Army bugle. In a moment the clear, quick notes of "Assembly" floated out across the valley.

"Just everybody stand easy," Fitzpatrick said. "We'll do this fair and easy, like always."

Allen's men answered the bugle call, and from down the creek below the den came six more inhabitants of the den. Louis was standing apart, on the edge of the group. Munson pointed at him with his rifle. "He gets no vote in this. That's the law here."

"Bliffert thought that one up," Fitzpatrick said. "I'm changing it. The nigra gets to vote."

Some of the miners cheered. They would have cheered anything, Hale thought, for they suddenly had a holiday occasion, a break after the grim winter. He was glad there was no whiskey to turn the affair into a real hell-binder. As it was, things were not good, by any means. Munson looked as if he were in a hanging mood, while Fitzpatrick's wild and ragged men were ready for anything.

Fitzpatrick stood on the stump. "The

Miners' Court of Spanish Creek is now in session. Bring the defendant before the bar!"

"Where at is the bar?" a man said. "I wish I could find one." He drew a big laugh.

"Now there's a man with good sense," Fitzpatrick said, and then he yelled: "Order in the court, god damn it!"

They shoved Hale before the stump.

"How do you plead?" Fitzpatrick asked.

"Not guilty. I'm. . . ."

"Not guilty, *Your Honor.*"

Hale wanted to kill the judge, but he repeated the words, nearly choking on them.

"That's better. We do things right around here. Now the fact seems to be that you were jumping the legal claims. . . ."

"I was not jumping anything! All the man had to do was tell me to leave. . . ."

"Shut up! One more bleat and I'll hold you in contempt of the whole damned outfit!"

"He was driving a stake on Mitchell's claim, not ten feet from the pile of rocks that marks the northeast corner," Munson said.

Fitzpatrick scratched his beard. "Is that true, Hale?"

"I didn't see any pile of rocks."

"Did you look?"

"Yes! But it looked like a game trail. No

footprints in it, and nothing to show there ever had been."

"I can understand that," Fitzpatrick allowed. "Munson's boys ain't been very sociable for some time." The miners laughed. Fitzpatrick held up his hand for silence, grinning. "Did you ask the eminent recorder of this district if there was open ground on that creek?"

"The way he runs things, he wouldn't know that there was even a creek there," Hale said angrily.

"That's a pure fact," one of Allen's men agreed.

Again there was laughter. Giles's hot, brooding eyes watched Hale with a glazed expression.

"It appears to me that you're sort of guilty of the charge as specified," Fitzpatrick said. "I now call for the jury to vote. Them that say he ain't guilty step down toward the creek. Them that say he is guilty step up the hill."

Munson was the first to move, up the hill. He was followed by everyone else. Ed Allen hesitated, and then he, too, joined those voting for conviction. Louis was already on the uphill side. He stayed where he was.

"That takes care of that," Fitzpatrick said. The whole thing was incredible. It was unreal, Hale thought. An innocent man simply could not be railroaded so swiftly. His sense of justice cried out against the entire farce. They were grinning at him, like it was a big joke of some kind. In a minute or two Fitzpatrick would announce that it *was* a joke, and then the whole performance would dissolve in uproarious laughter.

"Before I pronounce the sentence, are there any lies you've thought up in your defense?" the judge asked.

Hale shook his head.

"Munson? Anything more to add?"

There was a small crack of uncertainty now in Munson's gaunt expression. "I suppose he could have made a mistake, being new here."

"He's already convicted!" Peters, the bugler, shouted. "Let's get on with the punishment. Hang the bastard!"

"Banish him from the district!"

"Fifty kisses from Sweet Nellie!"

Fitzpatrick bellowed for order. "Giles, as foreman of the jury, what do you say?"

"Banishment from the district."

"That's proper," Fitzpatrick agreed. He put on an air of great judicial wisdom. "Of course, Munson says he could have made an honest mistake."

"Hang the bastard!" Peters said.

Hale marked the bugler well. Peters's beard was little more than fuzz. He could not be more than eighteen or nineteen, but the war had taught Hale that the very young often were the most cold-blooded and violent of all. He would remember Bugler Peters.

"My sentence is twenty lashes," Fitzpatrick announced.

"He's got to be banished," Giles protested.

"I have the authority. I am the judge. Twenty lashes is the sentence!"

Even when men grabbed him and dragged him, struggling and cursing, to a crossbar for hanging game, Hale still held a shred of belief that it was all a monstrous joke. He butted one man in the face. He lifted himself off the ground while his arms were held, and kicked a second man in the belly with both feet. Someone rapped him sharply with a gun barrel on the head. His senses reeled, but he still tried to fight while they bound his hands to the crossbar and tied his feet, widespread, to the trees that held it. They ripped his shirt and underwear from his back. Now he knew it was no joke.

It was supreme indignity to be hanging there like the lowest kind of felon. He twisted his head to look behind him. The men had fallen silent now. He saw faces

202

staring at him with strange, feral expressions. Peters's mouth was open, and his eyes were bright with anticipation. Giles was holding a braided whip. The first lash across his back was cracking fire. He saw the tip of Sweet Nellie curl clear around under his arm and fall away from his chest.

"That was a poor lick!" Peters yelled.

"I'll do better," Giles said. "There's lots of time." He grunted, as if in the act of swinging the second blow. Hale tensed against it, but the whip did not fall just then. "No use to bunch up your muscles like that," Giles said, as if giving sympathetic advice. "It's easier if. . . ." And then the second blow, and Hale ground his teeth. They could kill him, but he would not give them the satisfaction of hearing him cry out.

"Sentence suspended!" Fitzpatrick yelled.

There was a dead silence for an instant, and then a disappointed, animal growl of protest from the crowd.

"You can't do that!" Peters protested.

"I'm the judge, god damn you! You question my right to run this court, Peters, and we'll see what Giles can do to that lily-white back of yours! Sentence suspended. Release the man."

They turned him loose. With his upper clothing hanging in shreds, Hale stared at them, trying to study them face by face, but he was nearly blind with rage. The faces became one big blob to be hated without separation. All he could think of at the moment was to get his guns and begin to kill.

He heard someone mutter: "The first excitement around here in two weeks, and Fitzpatrick has to get softhearted."

"Old Aaron wouldn't've backed up."

"The defendant can now resume his original claim," Fitzpatrick said, "and it is hoped that the small punishment he has received will be sufficient warning to keep him from trying to jump the claims of other men."

"I bought that claim," Giles said.

"Return his money. One dollar, wasn't it?"

"It was a legal sale!"

"You've never been on the other end of Sweet Nellie, have you, Giles?" Fitzpatrick's voice was smooth and cold.

Hale was walking away when a dollar struck him and fell to the ground, clinking on a rock. He held his head high and kept on walking. Most of the blood heat had cooled in him before he reached the jutting hill, but it had been replaced by a deep, abiding feeling of outrage and a cold desire to send to hell everyone who had been at the den.

Munson and Louis were walking behind him.

Reason slowly overcame part of Hale's feelings. Louis could not have done other than act as he had, and Munson had had no way of knowing who Hale was. It had been a miserable, degrading mess, but neither Louis nor Munson could be held responsible.

Hale turned up the trail beside the branch creek. Louis went on toward his camp, while Munson followed Hale. Walking through the firs, Hale took a silver quarter from his watch pocket. When they reached the place where his gun belt lay, Munson was close behind him.

"When you pick that up, don't worry about putting it on." Munson cocked the rifle. "Just take it and walk away straight down the trail."

It was time for them to talk, time for Hale to identify himself, but caution was still his watchword. It held him just a few moments beyond the time when he was ready to present his credentials, and, during that brief period, he saw Munson glance at the trees ahead, and Hale took from the quick look a knowledge that Munson had not intended him to have.

"Pick it up carefully," Munson said.

Kneeling, with his hand on the ground, Hale opened his fist long enough for Munson to see the quarter, and then Hale shoved it into the needle mat. He picked up his gun belt and turned away, but not before the startled expression on Munson's face told him what he wanted to know.

As he went down the trail, Hale heard Munson talking to someone.

It was only a common quarter. Hale had studied it edgewise and on both sides, and he had never determined what the mark was that would identify him as a man sent by Ezekiel Blaine.

Louis walked slowly into Hale's camp when Hale was trying to wash his back.

"I didn't ask for help, and you can go to hell before I do, Brother Jones."

"You're going to get it anyway." Louis took the cloth from Hale's hand. He put a jar of Dr. Baldwin's Magic Ointment on the rocks beside the fire site. His touch was gentle. "That first one is mainly a big welt. The second one dug in pretty good. How would you have stood up to the full twenty?"

"None of your business."

Louis tossed the washcloth back into the gold pan of warm water and soap. He applied the ointment. "This works good on the legs of mules, so it ought to do for you."

"What's your business here, Louis?"

"Not too loud, please. I don't think that man's across the creek any more, but I'm not sure. Maybe they figure they can't watch us every minute."

"What's your business, Louis?"

"I want a man. I'm beginning to think he isn't here."

"That all?" Hale heard the metal lid scraping on the jar. He turned to face Louis.

"Truth," Louis said. "I don't think he's here."

"You're going to leave?"

"Not for a while."

Hale hunched his shoulders. The cool of the shade felt good on his tortured back, but the ointment was beginning to burn like lime.

"Did you ever see any of these men down there before?" Louis asked.

"No."

"I have. Four of them, for sure. Army deserters."

"Whose army?"

Louis put his back to the fire, looking across the creek. "Near Fort Hays last summer I saw ten deserters out on the prairie." He motioned with his hand toward the den. "Four of them are down there now."

"How can you remember that well?"

"That's the biggest part of my work. I remember not only faces, but the way a man walks and rides, the way he uses his hands, the tone of his voice."

"Fitzpatrick?" Hale asked.

"He was the sergeant. Giles was the corporal. Peters was there with his bugle. The one they call Jumpy was there, too, and maybe others that I didn't get a good look at today."

"They must have recognized you, too."

"No. They never saw me. I lay in the tall grass on top of a hill. They went by within fifteen feet of me, laughing, cursing General Custer, talking about all the gold they were going to find out here. They rode away in uniform, Army horses marked U.S., guns . . . everything. I understand more than five hundred men deserted the Seventh Cavalry like that."

"Are you after Army deserters, Louis?"

"There's no money in that. Let the Army catch them if it can. If they happen to be men I want for other reasons, yes, I'll take them." Louis shook his head. "There's no one in Fitzpatrick's bunch that I want." He turned to look at Hale. "Now, what's your business here?"

"It isn't preaching, like you told Fitzpatrick."

Louis grinned. "Did I do that?" He shrugged. "I can't blame you for not telling me. A man can get his throat cut pretty quick over a little gold, can't he?"

Hale stared at him.

"Or as much as you came to take out of here for Blaine."

"Let's hear some more about this mythical job," Hale said.

"There's a word I always liked. Mythical."

"You've learned a lot of words, Louis . . . and strange ideas."

"It bothers you that I can read and write, doesn't it? You think I ought to act and talk like a banjo-dancing nigger from your daddy's big plantation, don't you?"

"That isn't what we're talking about."

"No. And you don't want to talk about it, either, Mister Roy Hale, Southern gentleman. No, you don't."

"Damn you, Louis! You're always starting a big argument over something that you and I didn't create. You were born black and I was born white, and neither of us had a thing to say about it, and now. . . ."

"Yeah, now. Who does the saying now?"

"I didn't make this world, Louis. I didn't bring your father from Wolof country and put him in slavery. My father freed most of his slaves before the war, and they stayed right with him."

"You didn't make the world. That's a sorry answer."

Hale could see the anger in the man struggling with his strong intelligence. There must be times when Louis seethed with the torment of the damned. Hale himself had just borne the cross of injustice, but a Negro was never free of it.

Louis took a deep breath. His nostrils flared and he exhaled with a sigh, and with it some of the bitterness left him. "You almost understand, Hale. That's why we quarrel."

They were silent for a while. Although Hale's back was hurting badly, the greatest injury was to his pride as a human being. It was the greatest indignity he had ever suffered. Step by step he kept reviewing it.

"Fitzpatrick watched Munson," Louis said. "When he pronounced sentence and they dragged you away, he never took his eyes from Munson."

Of course. Fitzpatrick had never lost any of his suspicions about Hale's purpose in Spanish Creek. Even when Munson marched Hale to the den, accusing him of claim jumping, Fitzpatrick must have laughed inside, convinced that it was no more than a clumsy effort to disavow Hale. But when it went right on to the punishment with Sweet Nellie, Munson had not protested. He had been willing to stand there and let Hale take twenty lashes. The thought surely must have crossed Fitzpatrick's mind then that a man with his back cut to bloody shreds would be of no use to Munson. As Hale saw it, the price of deception had been mighty steep.

That had not been his idea when he started to stake a claim on the branch creek. He was sure the Southerners were up there some place, and he had wanted an excuse to get closer to them. Then Munson had taken him at face value, and he had gotten too damned close in a hurry.

Deception, huh? One of Ezekiel Blaine's words. All Hale had gotten out of it to date was two soul-searing licks from Sweet Nellie, but maybe Fitzpatrick had been fooled. Just a little.

"At least you learned two important things today," Louis said. "You know who you have to see to make your plans about the gold." He walked away.

"What's the second thing?"

Louis did not look back. "What it feels like to be tied up and lashed."

VII

Although he did not care if he ever moved another pound of gravel on his claim, Hale knew he would have to resume work on it in a day or two in order to maintain his rôle as a miner, but for a while he intended to use his sore back as an excuse to do something else. He built a chair like Louis's; he tinkered around his camp, brought spruce boughs from across the creek for a mattress, and improved his fire pit.

As for Munson, let him make the next move.

Louis and Allen's men were hard at work, and, down near the den, the miners were working their sluices. In the middle of the morning Fitzpatrick came striding up the creek. He visited with Allen's men, and then, looking too cheerful to let live, he came on up to Hale.

He saw Hale's expression and spread his hands. "What could I do? It was the law, and you heard the vote. They wanted to run you out. At least I saved you from that, and then I did the best I could about the lashes. I didn't want to see you banished."

"Why?"

Fitzpatrick seemed surprised. "You've got a claim. Maybe it hasn't been much so far, but you've still got a good chance to strike it. I figured you'd want to stay."

"Hell," Hale said disgustedly, "I'd leave right now if I felt like traveling. Even if Louis says a man couldn't get over the pass now, because of that last snow."

Fitzpatrick nodded. "He's right."

"Yeah. I noticed he voted right yesterday, too."

Again Fitzpatrick spread his hands. "What could he have done? Only Munson could have stopped it by begging you off or by dropping the charge."

"I'll see him in hell, along with your good friend, Giles."

"Ah, you'll feel better in a few days."

"How's the other way out of here?" Hale asked. "The Big Bayou route."

Fitzpatrick shook his head. "There's a pass there, too, not like Terrible, but it still catches lots of snow. It'll be two weeks, maybe more, before anyone could break through there."

"Lowe got out."

That bothered Fitzpatrick. Lowe, Hale had learned, had been one of Allen's group. "He was a damned fool for even trying."

"But he made it. Which way is this other pass?"

Fitzpatrick pointed. "I wouldn't try it."

"I think I'll go up this afternoon and take

213

a look to see if I can get mules across it."

Fitzpatrick shrugged. "Suit yourself. I'll bet you a quarter that one glance will turn you right around." He went on to visit Louis.

That afternoon Hale walked up the valley, through melting snow banks in timber that ran clear across the narrowing upper end, and on to where he could see the pass. The crest was not more than two miles away by his estimate, and that checked with what he had seen on Blaine's map. The pass began on open snow, then narrowed and ran on to the summit through dense timber. He tried the first snow bank with a pole. It was just a little less than his own height, six feet. Well, he had not expected anything better.

He did not return by the valley. Instead, he went into the aspens on the north side and ascended the mountain for about a quarter of a mile, then turned back toward camp. He had decided not to wait for Munson to come to him; he was going to call on the Southerners in their own lair. He had his rifle with him, on the chance that he would see a deer, and he had taken his pistol, too, because he did not want to leave it at his camp. It was easy traveling along the skirt of the mountain, but he saw no deer, or even a track.

His first glimpse of Munson's camp, seen from above, gave him the impression of a fort. For about 200 feet on the uphill side all the trees had been cut away, and they had been cleared for a lesser distance in front of the long, log structure. He started boldly down the hill.

Smoke puffed from the back wall of the cabin. A bullet drove into the damp leaf mold off to the side of Hale. "Hey!" he shouted, and raised both hands. A few moments later Munson appeared at one end of the cabin and signaled him on in by waving a rifle.

When he was close, Hale saw the right loopholes all the way along the back wall of the structure. There was a string of them in front, also. It was really three small cabins under a common roof of poles and earth, each structure separated by about ten feet, the open spaces piled with firewood, tools, and parts of saddles.

A second rifle was looking at Hale from the doorway of the middle cabin, held by a thin-faced man with a raggedly chopped red beard.

"Leave your weapons on the woodpile there," Munson ordered. He was not quite as rough as the day before, but he was certainly not accepting Hale as an ally.

The red-bearded man stepped back as they entered the room. Like the den, it had a low ceiling, heavy log walls — and an odor. And, also like the den, there was a man lying in a bunk, coughing. He roused up and sat on the edge of the bunk.

"All right," Munson said, "what were you doing up there on the hill?"

My God, was it going to start all over again? Munson had seen that quarter. What was wrong? "I was hunting," Hale said. "Don't tell me I can't hunt where I please."

The red-bearded man peered out one of the loopholes. "There hasn't been a deer back there since last October. I told you it was going to start, Steve. Now we've got to. . . ."

"I'll handle it," Munson said. "Hunting, eh?"

"They stopped at two lashes," the man on the bunk said. "Isn't that enough evidence, Munson?" He walked across to look out one of the front loopholes.

In the light streaming through the aperture, Hale saw lank, bearded cheeks with red spots burning high in them. The man was young, but the face was scrolled like old ivory. Two more men came in, both carrying rifles. One of them was tall and gaunt like Munson. His face was hard with suspicion. The other looked as if he belonged somewhere else, for he was chunky, deeply tanned, clean-shaven, and healthy-looking.

Five of them, Hale thought. *The sixth must be on guard down the trail.*

"It won't be good enough for me just to have you take him back to the bastards a second time," the red-haired man said.

"I said I'd handle it, Wilson." Munson pointed to the chunky man. "Get back to your post, Mitchell. You, too, Cochrane." Munson's tone carried the quality of long command that allows itself no doubt about being obeyed.

Mitchell and Cochrane barely hesitated before walking out.

"If we start it," Munson told the others, "all the months of waiting will be wiped out with the first shot."

"I'm ready," Wilson said. "Let's kill him."

The man at the loophole nodded. "Maybe we've waited too long for. . . ." He did not finish. "I stand with Wilson."

"You always were bloodthirsty, Becker," Munson said mildly, "but it's not going to be that way. I'm walking him out of here a second time." He gave them no chance to argue further.

In the areaway Hale said: "My guns?"

"Leave them right there." Munson mo-

217

tioned him down the trail.

Not far below the cabin they passed a place where for fifty feet along the creek on both sides muddy ashes and piles of gravel were mixed. It was the only place where Hale saw any considerable amount of mining. They must have burned tons and tons of wood there during the winter, but there was no evidence of any recent activity.

"You found that quarter, didn't you?" Hale asked.

"Keep walking."

Close to where Hale had been surprised the first time, a man stepped out from concealment among a close-growing clump of firs. "So you got him a second time, Munson." Young, with long blond hair falling over his ears, the trail guard was a clear-eyed youngster who, like the man called Mitchell, appeared to have wintered well.

"Go on up and take the rock post, Bentley," Munson said. "Tell Cochrane to relieve me here in two hours."

"But I've only been. . . ."

Munson cut him off with an unhurried gesture that said: "Go!"

Bentley did not argue about it.

Munson's vigilant attitude was now somewhat relaxed, but he still held his rifle in handy position as he studied Hale. "Do you have a mineral glass?"

"I don't know what you mean."

"A magnifying glass."

Hale shook his head. "Why?"

Some decision in Munson's mind hung in the balance, and then the scales tipped toward caution and suspicion. He pointed with the rifle down the trail.

"If you couldn't find that quarter, I can show you right where . . . ," Hale began.

"Get out."

"What about my guns?"

"I'll think about that. Get out."

Hale had no choice. After a short distance he cut to his left and stayed in the trees until he reached his camp. Twice now he had made contact with the men he had come to serve. The first time he had been beaten with a whip for his pains, and the second time the Southerners had wanted to kill him.

The whole bunch could go to hell before he would make another effort to talk to them.

While he was getting ready to make biscuits, he found the elk steak that someone had left in his Dutch oven. It was big enough for two men, and it was probably poisoned, he thought, and then he laughed at himself for holding such an idea. His temper resumed an even keel, and he began to reason out the situation he had found at Munson's fort. The Southerners must have felt they were under siege all winter, not knowing what was going to happen from day to day. Trapped by the snow, slaves to their own wealth, fearful of everyone else in Spanish Creek, they must have passed a tense winter up there in the gloom on the shady side of the valley. In spite of all that, they apparently had worked the placer where all the ashes and charred ends of wood were intermingled with the gravel.

As Ezekiel Blaine had pointed out, the men in the big cabin down on the creek had been content to loaf and let others pile up gold. No wonder Munson and his men were now living with suspicions strained to the breaking point. Munson had found that quarter, sure enough — an ordinary, rather worn 1858 Liberty-and-Eagle two-bit piece. It should have been enough to tell him that Hale had been sent by Blaine, but no — Munson was so steeped in worry and distrust that he had to have a magnifying glass to look for some secret mark on the coin.

He had almost accepted Hale there on the trail just after sending the guard away. For a moment he had been on the verge of talking, and then he had retreated into distrust. The fact that not one of the other Southerners had shown Hale anything but hostility indicated that Munson had not told them about the quarter, and that meant that he was not trusting even his own men. A winter of cabin fever and a pile of gold could give any man a rather bleak and deadly view of friends, let alone enemies.

I wonder where they've cached their gold?

Hale saved half the steak to be warmed over for breakfast. He found a cigar only partly broken and was smoking that and drinking coffee, sitting in his crude chair like the king of Spanish Creek, when Allen came from across the creek.

Allen warmed his hind-side at the fire. "Did you try the steak?"

"Very good. Thanks."

There was something on Allen's mind, but he was not rushing to get it said. "Treherne and Millerton got that elk. First one we've had for two weeks."

"I hunted up the valley this afternoon, but I never even saw a track."

"Yeah. It's like that sometimes." Allen was silent for a time. "It wouldn't have done much good for me and the boys to vote the other way, Hale. We used to try it, but there never were enough of us."

"So you just go with the sons-of-bitches to get along?"

Allen turned red. "That's about it, I guess."

"Anything goes, just so you aren't bothered. You kiss Fitzpatrick's. . . ."

"We've got to take care of ourselves! We want to hold out until enough honest men come in here to make this a safe, decent district. Damn it, Hale, you can understand. . . ."

"No, I can't understand at all. It would be a hell of a world if we all sat on our butts waiting for honest men to save us. How much gold have you got hidden over there in your camp, Allen?"

Allen gave Hale a quick, startled look. "Some, of course."

"Enough to worry about, huh?" Hale knew there was no point in assailing Allen, but he took one last dig. "Maybe all the fine honest men you're waiting for will get here a little too late to save your gold for you."

"I know. We've talked about that. What do you suggest we ought to do?"

He had come over for help, and he had received a browbeating. The world was full of Allens — solid citizens voting for right and justice when the odds were with them, silent when they were badly outnumbered.

Hale was not out to reform society, so he modified his harsh tone. "You could throw in with Munson's men."

"Uhn-uh." Allen shook his head. "We tried that late last fall, when we realized how bad things were. They didn't trust us. They've struck it so rich on that little creek that they won't trust anyone."

"How do you know they've struck it rich?"

"They burned hundreds of cords of wood up there most of the winter, melting the snow, thawing the ground, while the rest of us huddled in our cabins, playing cards and going crazy. Munson's boys wouldn't have been working like that for any trifling two-bits a pan."

"Have you got a mineral glass?"

Allen produced a small, metal-shielded object. "Keep it as long as you need it." He glanced toward Louis's camp. There was a fire before the lean-to, but no sign of Louis. All four mules were standing near the creek.

"What happened to Bliffert?" Hale asked.

"Giles got him with a knife."

"Why?"

Allen hesitated. "Aaron Bliffert was the leader of that bunch. They were sort of split about trying to take the Southerners' gold by straight-out force or waiting until Munson tried to get out with it. Bliffert was for

223

war. Fitzpatrick and some of the others said to wait. Fitzpatrick was arguing with Bliffert about it when Giles settled it with a knife in the liver."

"How do you know all that?" Hale asked.

"Up until the time the snow started to go, some of us used to visit down there. Even Munson's men came down . . . no more than one at a time, though."

"And those facts were openly stated to you."

"Not exactly openly," Allen said. "We just sort of put one thing and another together. Of course, they wouldn't have said it right out to any of us."

Hale rose. "I've got to check my mules."

Allen went with him. There was no one in Louis's camp. They were on their way back, with Hale leading Molly, when Allen at last got around to what he had come to say.

"Some of us want you to take our gold out, Hale. When you and Louis first got here, we figured you'd been sent in to carry gold for Munson. Now we know better, but we still figure you're the man who can do it. We'll pay ten percent of everything you carry, just like any express."

"How much will that be?"

Allen hesitated. "The first thing is, will you do it?"

"You never saw me before. Why are you willing to trust me?"

"We're desperate." Allen hastened to qualify the remark. "I don't mean that like it sounds. What I mean is, we know we can't wait too much longer. Not all of us are in agreement on this, but four of us are. Will you do it?"

"What qualifies me to get out any more than one of your own men?"

"For one thing, you've got mules. We ate ours last winter. The main thing is, you're tough."

Hale grunted. "You've got the wrong man, Allen. I came here to mine, not to get myself killed trying to save someone else's gold."

They reached Hale's camp. He tied Molly near his tarpaulin lean-to. It seemed incredible that men could be so frightened and so distrustful of each other that they could not get together, take their miserable gold, walk out of Spanish Creek, and tell Fitzpatrick in advance that they were going. There were ten men in the Allen camp and six with Munson, with perhaps no more than twenty opposed to them. With less than sixteen men, Hale had gone through Yankee lines and made the blue-bellies like it.

"You could do it," Allen urged. "We could load your mule by night. With only ten minutes' start, how could anyone on foot catch you?"

"Snow," Hale said. "They'd catch up. Why do you think the mules haven't been bothered? Louis and I were more than an hour getting them through some of the drifts we struck. Don't think Fitzpatrick didn't notice the crust cuts clear up on the chests of the mules. Don't talk to me about making a fast run out of here, Allen."

"I still think it could be done. You'd need a bigger head start, is all." Allen had been holding back another bit of information. "We've got a man with Fitzpatrick's bunch. He'd be able to tell us if they were on to the time you were starting. If they knew, we could hold off until another time, but eventually it would work."

"Eventually your ass. No, thanks," Hale said.

"Well, keep thinking about it."

"Who's your man down there in the den?"

"Uhn-uh. Only about half my own bunch knows about him, and that's the best way to keep it."

Gold, Hale thought. It spread its infection worse than cholera. He himself had not found enough to plate a small needle, but he was beginning to hate the very name of the yellow metal.

"Don't say no," Allen pleaded. "Think about it." Once more he hesitated. "It would mean about two thousand dollars in your pocket." He walked away.

The devil! So Allen and three others had around $20,000 of the stuff, not even counting the other seven men in his camp. Hale watched Allen go across the creek, and then he looked up and down the valley. It had been a beautiful, peaceful place. For Indians.

He had two more visitors that evening.

He did not hear or see the first one until Molly minced around uneasily and indicated him with her ears set like a gunsight.

Louis came out of the trees. "You went hunting with a rifle and a pistol," he said. "You came back rather defenseless, didn't you?"

"You see too much, Louis."

"I also read tracks." Louis smiled. "They've got a pretty stout outpost up there, haven't they?"

"I'd say so. What else did you see on your prowl?"

"That's about all." Louis put his rifle on Hale's bed, and then he went on to his camp.

"Thanks."

Louis waved without looking back.

227

Molly gave a warning on the second visitor, also. That was in the dark, perhaps midnight, Hale guessed.

Like the mule, he had heard this one coming. He was not sleeping under the canvas now. After the fire died down, he had moved his bed back into the trees. He lifted Louis's rifle quietly and waited.

The man went to the front of the lean-to. "Hale! Hale!" he called in a hoarse whisper. It was Steve Munson.

"Over here." Hale heard the quick scuff of the man's feet as he swung around.

"Hale?"

"Here, damn it!"

Munson came over to him. Even then he was not completely sure. He knelt and said: "Let me feel your back." He ran his fingers across the back of Hale's shirt. "You're bleeding, man."

"I rolled on my back in my sleep. What do you want?"

"I've decided you're the right man. I can't even read the date on that quarter, and Mitchell has lost his mineral glass, but maybe. . . ."

"Let's get it right." Before crawling in, Hale had emptied his pockets. He fumbled inside one of his boots near the head of the bed and got the magnifying glass and a waterproof container of matches.

By the light of a match shielded under the teepee of a blanket, Munson studied the quarter with the glass. The match burned out, and he said: "Light another one. Damn, but my eyes have failed in the last year!"

The second match was enough. "Yeah!" Munson said. "See that diagonal scratch across the upper part of the shield on the eagle? That's it."

With his naked eye, Hale could see the mark, as well as others all over the coin. "Why couldn't one of your men see it?" The match burned his fingers. He dropped it and rubbed it out on the blanket.

"I guess you're Blaine's courier, sure enough."

Munson had ignored Hale's question. The answer was that he had not shown the coin to his companions.

"Now, how about Louis?" Munson asked.

"He's not in this. Don't worry about him."

"I worry about everybody. That's why we're still alive." Munson rose and peered around at the night. "What about him, I asked."

Rather than argue, Hale said: "He's with me."

"All right then, since he's your man. . . . Well, all right. What's Blaine's plan to move the gold?"

"That's up to me."

"No plan?" Munson was letdown. "I thought Blaine would have something foolproof worked out. We all did. Just talking about it all winter helped us to keep going. Now you say there isn't any plan at all."

"There will be," Hale said. "How much is there to handle?"

"Around fifty thousand."

Christ! Things were getting worse all the time. "What's the weight?"

"Between one fifty and one seventy. At first we had a wooden balance that Wilson had whittled out. We used Bentley's watch on one side because we knew it weighed just six ounces. He'd had it on a gold scales one night in Denver. But then he lost the watch in the creek one morning. . . . We just sort of guessed after that. It didn't make much difference, anyway, since . . . I've got to get back. I left the trail post to come down here."

"Just a minute. We've got to work out a few details. First, where are you keeping the gold?"

"I'll let you know about that at the proper time."

"Look, Munson, the minute I start up the trail to your fort, with mules, what do you

230

think is going to happen?"

"I *know* what will happen if you try that. I'll work out the plan and let you know later."

"Get it straight," Hale said. "I'm the one who's going to set the plan."

"It's our gold. You'll do as I say." Munson's quiet statement went beyond authority; it verged on mania. He moved off into the darkness.

One winter in Spanish Creek was too much for any man, Hale thought.

Now Hale had not only Fitzpatrick's thugs and murderers to handle, but a stubborn, power-hugging Southerner as well. He must have been out of his mind when he walked out on Sara Perkins to take this job.

VIII

Three days of warm weather made Hale uneasy, for he knew the snow would be melting on the passes, and as yet he had received no plan from Munson, or even another visit. If Munson was making plans up there in the fort, he was keeping them very quiet.

Hale was back at work on his claim, still pretending to be a miner. Nothing had changed; it was strictly labor, the rocks as heavy as ever, the water even colder than

231

before. He enlarged his test hole, sticking close to the beaver run in order to undermine the willows. He still had Allen's glass. Now and then he was able to see a speck of gold with it, and once he recovered a flake and examined it on his thumbnail. It jumped into largeness under the magnifying glass, but, when he squinted at it with the naked eye, he wondered how in Tophet the Southerners had ever accumulated a 160 pounds of the miserable stuff.

Fitzpatrick came by on his daily spying tour and was heartily encouraging. "A man never knows when he's close to gold until he finds it. Patience, Major." Fitzpatrick looked at the sky. "Anyway, it's wonderful digging weather that gives a man a feeling of goodness and joy." From all appearances, Fitzpatrick, of the fine golden beard and twinkling eye, was just a friendly miner, interested in the welfare and success of everyone in Spanish Creek.

The only consolation Hale got out of the work was that the sun on his back made his healing cuts feel better, but, when he rolled on them in his sleep, he still had a curse for Giles and everyone else at the den.

Louis came down to visit everyday.

"If your man's not here, what's keeping you around?" Hale asked.

"I'm thinking."

"Have you thought far enough to take my offer to come in with me on the job?" Sometime before, Hale had dropped all pretense with Louis.

"No plan yet?"

Hale leaned on his shovel. "I'm thinking. Half the money, Louis. Five hundred dollars. That's cleaner money than you get for collecting heads."

"Is it? What makes you think *you* won't have to collect a few heads before you ever get clear with that gold? Any way you want to twist it, you're going to kill for money."

It was an interpretation that Hale had not considered. He saw the truth of it, but he was not going to foredoom himself by arguing logic with Louis Jones. "Are you with me?"

"Still thinking." Louis studied the sky. "I'll bet you four ounces of coffee it snows before nightfall."

"You just lost a quarter of a pound of coffee."

It was Hale who lost. Before sundown the storm slanted in from the east, and for an hour huge, wet flakes fell thickly.

In the middle of the storm Allen slushed into Hale's camp and joined him under the canvas shelter. Hale gave him a cup of strong tea. "I just lost the last bean from my coffee sack, betting Louis it wouldn't snow today."

"He predicted it?" Allen asked quickly, and, when Hale nodded, Allen said: "I wish we had known that. Do you suppose he can do it again, for sure?"

"I don't know. Why?"

"Frank Millerton and Henry Treherne have made up their minds. They're going to make a run for it. Lowe went out in a snowstorm and made it, so they figure they can do the same. They want to make their start before the storm, because these late snows don't stay on the ground very long.

"They've made snow-webs . . . a kind of snowshoe . . . and tried 'em out on their hunting trips. They know just how to go around the guard at the foot of Woody Pass, and once they're over the top. . . ."

"There's a guard?"

"For the last four days," Allen said. He jerked his thumb toward Terrible Pass. "Another one up there, day and night."

"Your men have seen them?"

"No. But I told you we know what's going on."

"Yeah. Your man in Fitzpatrick's den."

Allen nodded. "I'm going up and see Louis."

■ ■ ■ ■

The next morning the snow was gone two hours after the sun rose. Reluctant to work, Hale considered faking another hunting trip in order to look over the guard post at the foot of Woody Pass, but he decided it might help alert the man there; it was better to stay away from Woody Pass until after Millerton and Treherne were clear.

He dug in his test pit and was surprised in the afternoon to see a small streak of gold in his pan. It was so little that he did not try to save it, but later, when the gold kept showing in every pan, he became interested. The outfitter in Silver Bell had tried to sell him a jar of mercury, explaining that it would amalgamate readily with gold, but Hale had thought the price and the weight too much.

Now he dumped the gold and the sand residue into an empty tomato can. At the end of the day he could hardly see anything in the bottom of the container. He showed it to Louis, who peered and peered and nodded gravely. "By fall you'll have enough to buy a new can of tomatoes."

They laughed about it, but it was short-lived humor, for Louis asked: "Allen told you about the two men?"

"Uhn-huh. What do you think about it?"

"It looks like snow again tonight." Louis gave Hale a long look. "We could help those men a little."

"It's their business."

"One of us could go up and kill that guard."

"They know how to get past him. If we kill the guard, the whole thing will blow up in our faces."

"Your face," Louis said. "I'm still thinking." Resentment was rising in him again. "They can kill anyone they want to, but we can't do anything like that. That's good, pure white man's thinking, Hale."

"Not white, not black, just human." Hale went back to his camp.

Just after dusk the snow began. Sometime before, Allen had gone to see Louis, returning to his own camp at a trot.

To Henry Treherne's and Frank Millerton's way of thinking, the snow could have not come at a more happily fortuitous time. They had had Louis's prediction about it, although anyone could have seen the signs this time. With snow-webs tied to their packs, their gold secure in buckskin pokes inside the packs, they went at a trot up the game trail on the south side of the valley. There was a shorter route that lay parallel to theirs, between them and the creek, but that was the way Fitzpatrick's men went to and from the foot of Woody Pass.

The wet snow was rapidly covering their tracks. That was a help, but the main value of the storm was the cover it would give them to go above and around the guard post. They were both young men, and they moved quickly. Frank Millerton was twenty-six, while Treherne was almost nineteen. They were both from the same small town in Ohio, and both had enough gold to realize their ambitions.

First, they would put their money in a Denver bank. Then they would draw $100 apiece and tear the town apart for a night or two. After that they would go back to Ohio together, Treherne to buy a farm, Millerton to marry his sweetheart.

"We made the break!" Treherne said. "Why did we stall so long, going batty in that camp, living like animals?"

"I was beginning to think like the others," Millerton said, "afraid of my own shadow."

They pushed on eagerly through snow that was fluffed in little mounds. Where their feet crushed it against the ground, it was cold gray slush. Not far from the pass they struck snow banks and put on their webs — clumsy contrivances they had made of peeled and steamed fir branches and criss-crossing scraps of leather. Heavy and awkward as the snowshoes were, they served their purpose well.

Where the timber thinned away before an open space at the foot of the pass, they stopped to look things over. The guard post, they knew, was 100 yards down to their left — a canvas shelter cleverly hidden in a clump of trees.

"We can't even see the trees," Treherne whispered, "so how can he see us?"

"He can't. That's the beauty of this storm."

Holding below massive cliffs that blocked them from going higher on the mountain, they snow-shoed into the pass.

After a quarter of a mile, stopping to rest, they grinned at each other. "We made it!" Treherne said.

The trees were close ahead, a dark, indistinct mass in the gloom of falling snow and coming night. A few minutes later Treherne said: "Hey! What kind of track is that? It looks like. . . ."

He never spoke again. A rifle flamed in the trees and a bullet struck him in the heart. Millerton was not as lucky. A heavy ball smashed his hip and left him shocked and nearly helpless, sprawled on his side, his rifle flung aside and buried in the snow. He began to crawl toward Treherne, who had a pistol in his belt. In spite of his impeding snowshoes, Millerton almost made it.

And then Peters, the bugler, came from the trees on snowshoes of his own. He fired one hasty shot that struck the prostrate man but did not stop him from continuing to drag himself toward Treherne. The second shot was at point-blank range into the staring, snow-wet face.

The second man in the trees was Amos Jordan, also once of the 7th Cavalry. He was slower than Peters getting into his webs, but he got there before Peters had gone through both packs. "Don't scatter that stuff around!" Jordan warned. "We'll just have to pick it up again to bury it." He began to rifle Millerton's pack.

Millerton stirred and groaned. He made a bubbling sound and tried to lift his shattered face from the snow.

"You son-of-a-bitch, Peters!" Jordan cried shrilly. "You didn't finish him!" Then he clubbed the wounded man with his pistol, and Millerton was still again.

They found seven heavy pokes of gold in the packs, hefted them, and estimated their value. "Don't worry about those," Jordan said. "Let's get to work." They used Treherne's webs to dig into the snow.

Millerton did not sink deep enough to suit Peters, so the young men walked back and forth on him to smash him down. Jordan saw the dying man open his eyes and move his hand. "Get off him!" Jordan screamed. He began to push snow into the hole, against Peters's legs and over Millerton's face.

They went back to their snow pit in the dark trees. Against orders, Peters broke small dead limbs from the trunks and built a tiny fire. "Seven of them, Jordan! Just feel that weight."

"You feel it."

Peters laughed. "It got to you, huh? Yelling like an old woman because he moved. You wasn't so squeamish about Blake, and that big one with all the pictures in his pack."

"That was daytime."

"Daytime, nighttime . . . gold weighs the same." Peters's eyes narrowed. "One poke for us, huh? We can't bury it by the. . . ."

"No! That bastard Fitzpatrick smells out everything. How did he know to move the guard post up here yesterday?"

"I could have figured that out myself. Any

fool could tell it was going to snow."

"He'll know just how many pokes they had, I tell you."

Peters was not listening. He had opened one of the pokes and was dipping the gold, grinning as he watched it spill from his fingers.

The snow went on for another hour. Sometime in the night, driven by terrifying thoughts that he could not overcome, Jordan went out on the snow. There was only a bumpy irregularity where they had done their work. Millerton had not clawed out of his grave.

The bugle blew "Assembly" late in the afternoon. Hale was staring into his gold pan. Unless he had lost his senses, he was looking at a whole string of nuggets the size of wheat grains. To hell with that bugle summons, he had work to do.

Louis came by and said: "We'd better go. It's always best to know what the enemy is doing." He watched soberly while Hale cast around for a place to hide his tomato can.

They overtook Allen's men going to the meeting.

"Did they make the run last night?" Hale murmured.

Allen nodded happily.

"Think they made it?"

"I'm sure of it." A little later Allen turned pale, when they all could see what appeared to be the figure of a man hanging from the crossbar near the den.

It was a man, and he had been hanged.

Fitzpatrick got on the stump. He did not have to call for silence. "It's a little late to vote on this case. The boys were awful upset when they caught him stealing gold from one of the sluices. I was down at the creek, and, before I could get back to hold a fair and legal trial, they'd hanged him. They voted solid for it, so I guess there's no sense in voting again, unless some of you want to. Allen?"

Allen's face was a ghastly study as he stared at the hanged man. He did not answer.

"Hale? How about you, Louis?"

"No vote," Louis said. He walked over close to the hanged man. "What was his name?"

"Jumpy Dutch," Fitzpatrick said. "He was a fine man until his appetite for gold got too big. Case closed then, gentlemen. Giles, enter the vote for guilty as unanimous."

"Fitzpatrick, you dirty, murdering son-of-a-bitch!" a man shouted. It was Ethan Holmes, one of Allen's men. He tugged at his pistol as he ran toward Fitzpatrick.

A den man who had been waiting for such an incident hit him with a club and knocked him senseless. Peters started to finish him with a pistol.

"Stop!" Fitzpatrick roared, and Peters put the pistol away. "The man was overwrought. As punishment for disturbing the deliberations of the court, I assign him to take charge of the burial detail."

The Allen men carried the body away in a canvas. After being revived, Holmes was no help. He could barely carry himself up the creek.

"Dutch was your man?" Hale asked Allen.

Allen nodded. He was stunned and terrified. "Holmes's cousin. He deserted the Army with Fitzpatrick and the others, but he wasn't a filthy murderer. He always let us know what was being planned, and he got away with it so long we quit worrying about him being caught."

Louis said: "He wasn't hanged. He was dead before that. Did you see how his fingers were broken and burned?"

Allen stared at him in mute horror. He nodded when Louis asked him if Dutch had known that Millerton and Treherne were going out.

"They still had a chance to make it," Hale

said. He met Louis's cold look defiantly.

Munson was standing on the jutting hill. "What kind of dirty business was that down there?" he yelled.

Hale left the others on the lower trail and went up to talk to him. For the first time Hale saw a fading of confidence in the grim, hollow-cheeked face when Munson heard the story.

"It's getting close, Hale, awful damned close."

"Yes, it is. Come down tonight and I'll tell you. . . ."

"I'm the one that will tell you! Don't try to get in touch with me. No one up there but me knows who you are. I've given orders that from now on no warning shots will be fired, like you got that time above our camp." Munson shouldered his rifle and went back up the trail.

Louis was waiting in Hale's camp. Someone had stacked both the riding saddle and the pack saddle on a pile of wood and built a fire. All the gear was now a smoking, stinking ruin.

"Same thing in my camp," Louis said. He spoke quietly, but he was the angriest man Hale had ever seen. Sometimes he had been sullen and sometimes he had appeared to be angry, but now there was a deep outrage in him that exuded from his whole being like a physical force. He looked toward the den and said: "I'm throwing in with you, Hale, split or no split."

Down in the den, Peters was asleep in the bunk. Walt was the only other man in the room. Everyone had expected him to die, but he had beaten the infection in his foot, and pneumonia as well.

Giles came in and said: "Hobble out of here, Walt."

"It smells better outside, anyway."

Giles roused Peters by pricking his throat with the point of a knife. "Two more pokes, Johnny-Blow-the-Bugle. You only turned in five."

Peters made a note of Jordan's betrayal. He also made a very practical assessment of the hair-smeared knife at his young throat, and the fact that Giles's eyes looked the way they did when he was whipping a man. He produced the pokes from behind a loose piece of chinking by his bunk.

"Now you can sleep with a clear conscience," Giles said. He slipped one of the bags under his shirt as he went across the room to the Jug, which sat in full view on a corner shelf. It was flint hide, the Jug, two thicknesses that had been soaked in water, then fire-dried full of fine sand to the shape of a huge, squatty bottle with a small neck. Then the sand had been dumped out and the fruits of the den men's labor poured at intervals down through the tight neck. That is, labor on lonely trails near Spanish Creek. What the den men mined as individuals was theirs to keep, as well as something to give them worried nights.

But the Jug was common property, and one day soon it would be opened with an axe and the contents evenly distributed to everyone. By keeping it in plain sight, Fitzpatrick had forestalled a lot of trouble. Familiarity breeds contempt. The Jug was there day and night. Everyone could watch his neighbor. No one had to speculate about what was happening to his share hidden in some secret place. All he had to do was look across the room, and there was the Jug.

Through the ruffled, funnel-shaped opening, down through the tight neck, Giles carefully poured the contents of the poke. He turned away, and from the edge of the doorway Fitzpatrick said jovially: "Now the other one, if you please."

"What other one?"

"Jumpy said it was seven."

Giles emptied the second poke into the Jug.

"I might have let you keep it," Fitzpatrick said, "but it could have inclined you toward being a thief, heaven forbid. Come on outside."

They went up the hill out of earshot of Walt and two others who were cutting firewood. "How much longer are we going to wait?" Giles asked.

"The same as always, until Munson tries to move it."

"Some of the boys are pretty edgy. They figure. . . ."

"I know! They're ready to tackle Munson, get about six men killed before breaking the place . . . and find nothing afterward. Jumpy didn't tell us where Allen's men keep their pokes, did he?"

"He would have, but he didn't know."

Fitzpatrick bobbed his head. "And maybe not everyone in Munson's camp knows where their stuff is. You could do four times to Munson what you did to Jumpy and never make him talk."

"Suppose they don't make a move before the valley is full of miners?"

"Ah, but they will, they will," Fitzpatrick said.

Giles gave him a tight, speculative look. "Have you bought somebody in Munson's camp?"

"What? Would I, Ewan Fitzpatrick, stoop to such low treachery?"

"Yeah," Giles said. It did not seem likely that one of the Southerners would betray his companions, but, living without faith of any kind, Giles had no faith in any human being. It just might be that Fitzpatrick had gotten to someone in Munson's bunch. "One thing . . . we'd better get rid of Hale and his black friend."

"*Tsk, tsk!* Those innocent miners?"

"Oh, hell, you know better than that!"

"No, I don't," Fitzpatrick said. "I have no final word on those two."

That statement reinforced Giles's guess about there being an informant in the Munson camp.

"Not that we won't watch Hale and Louis," Fitzpatrick said, "but we must do nothing to stain the spotless record of true justice that has always been the refuge of the innocent and oppressed in Spanish Creek." He went down the hill, laughing.

IX

Hale had struck it. It was a twist of events that both amazed and excited him. Every pan he washed was running from three- to four-inch strings of heavy gold, very often with nugget grains that ran, at a guess, an ounce to a pan. He put into the tomato can only a very little of his find. All the rest went into a buckskin poke that he kept in his pocket, until the growing bulk of it made a bulge that worried him. Someone might see it and guess his secret, so, while he was working, he kept the bag hidden in the rocks close by.

One night, when Louis was visiting him, Hale told him about the strike.

"Yes," Louis said. "I've noticed for the last three days that you've been working like a madman. Don't you realize that there's other eyes, besides mine, around here?"

"By Tophet! You're right. I'd better slow down." Hale tried to peer all around beyond the limits of the firelight. He saw Louis eyeing him strangely. "Oh, I know what you're thinking, but it really hasn't gotten to me, Louis. I still know why I'm here."

"Do you?" Louis's expression was harsh, demanding. "What have you done about Munson?"

"I told you it's up to him. Besides, the way it's been snowing. . . ." Hale stopped. He faced the truth, and the truth was that he had been wishing that Munson would announce that he had decided to outwit Fitzpatrick. The wish had grown stronger every time Hale saw gold in his pan.

Louis was reading his thoughts. "It can be a yellow bitch, Hale. Three men are dead of it just since we came."

"Three? You can't say Treherne and Millerton are dead."

"They are, I'm sure. When the snow melts, someone will find them in the narrow part of Woody Pass."

"How do you know?"

"I prowled up there this morning. There's a guard post in the first of the trees. Two men came down and two went up to relieve them." Louis shook his head gloomily. "You couldn't get through, even at night. You have to cross at least three hundred yards of open snow right in front of that guard post."

"Then we couldn't have gotten the guard when you suggested it?"

"No. Fitzpatrick was ahead of us. I still thought there was only one man at the bottom of the pass. You know what happened, don't you?"

"Yeah. Jumpy Dutch."

"He knew that Millerton and Treherne were going out. They tortured him, Hale. There were worse marks on his body than those broken fingers. He talked, and then they strangled him and put the rope around his neck and strung him up." The firelight gleamed in Louis's somber eyes. "He was eighteen years old."

"Giles?"

"I think so. I watched his face when he was whipping you. I think he's the one."

"If it comes to where we have no chance to get out, he's the one I want to take to hell with me first of all," Hale said bitterly.

"That's understandable." Louis looked across the fire. "And foolish. Don't let it color your thinking. We can get out, I'm almost sure, and we can take the mules, too." They both had been talking in very low voices, and now Louis's words barely reached across the flames. "On the dry, south side of the mountain I found an old Indian trail. It winds in and out of the rocks and it's steep, but, if the last part of it is no worse than what I've seen, we can make it." Louis described the route in detail.

"How about snow near the top?" Hale asked.

"As far as I can tell, the whole way lies on the south slope. I'll know after tonight."

"Why isn't it guarded?"

"They may not know about it. Up from the bottom for maybe a half mile, the aspens have overgrown everything, so there's no sign at all of a trail. But it's there, and I'll run out the rest of it tonight."

They could go any time after the trail

proved passable, Hale thought. He would have to get together with Munson, even against the man's orders, and force the decision. And then he thought of his claim, and the gold he had buried not five feet from where he was sitting.

He did not sleep well that night, thinking about Louis out in the starlight, thinking about his rich claim. Following his habit of never staying in the lean-to all night, he was back in the aspens when Munson came. As usual, Molly stomped around to give the alarm, but Hale was already awake.

"You came at the right time," Hale said. "Louis is almost sure we have the way to get out. If everything looks good, we can plan on tomorrow night or the night after that."

For once, Munson seemed to be listening instead of telling.

"Someone wrecked our saddles and panniers, but Allen has. . . ."

"No," Munson said. "Getting them there would tip it off. Too many men would know about it. I've got all that equipment."

"Good enough. Now, we'll figure on meeting you in the timber east of your cabins. Once we move the mules, I want to keep them moving. Understand? I don't want to waste more than five minutes while your men are loading the gold. If you and all your boys want to go with us. . . ."

"No," Munson said. "Becker has the lung fever. He couldn't make it, and I don't think Cochrane could, either. We're not going to desert them to be knocked on the head, so we'll all stay. I can hold out against an army up there, Hale."

Munson had been reasonable enough so far, but his last statement irked Hale. "If you can stand against an army, why don't you sit tight and outwait Fitzpatrick?"

"The gold has got to go out!"

"Why? At best, it's a big risk, and you say that. . . ."

"It'll be insured for eighty percent the minute it's in your hands. If they get you and the nigger before you've gone a hundred feet, Blaine will pay off eighty percent."

That made sense, all right, but it was not a happy thought. "You know Ezekiel Blaine that well?" Hale asked. "You trust him that much?"

"With my life!" Munson said. "But I'm beginning to wonder about you, Hale. Are you trying to worm out of the job he sent you to do? What kind of a cowardly . . . ?"

"I said I'd do the job, god damn it, and I will!"

"Good. There's just one detail I object to.

Forget this old Indian trail. You'll have to use Terrible Pass."

There it was again, the whole thing coming apart in the face of Munson's stubbornness. Hale was silent for a time, controlling his irritation. "There's a guard, maybe more than one, on Terrible Pass, and I'm sure the snow up high is still too much for the mules."

"I know about those guards. I've seen them. They can be handled. Mitchell and I will take care of them for you."

"Will you melt the snow ahead of us, too?"

"Then you'll just have to wait a while. I can hold out till the pass is open."

Hale's temper was getting away. Again he took a long silence before saying: "Why does it have to be Terrible Pass?"

"Because I say so."

A head-on argument with Munson was useless. Hale tried to wheel and come in on the flank. "It must have been a miserable winter up there in the snow, with never a chance to talk to anyone else in Spanish Creek. I suppose. . . ."

"We didn't pull a hole in after us, Hale. We visited around . . . one at a time, that is. We visited with Allen's boys and went down to Fitzpatrick's cabin. We figured nothing was going to happen as long as we were all snowed in. We worked and we got around to see how others were doing, so don't try to make out that I'm crazy from cabin fever."

Hale's subtle flank attack died a-borning. "I don't know why you keep insisting on Terrible Pass," he said.

"I do, though, and that's it." Munson rose from his sitting position. "Mitchell knows who you are. He's the only other one besides me that does. If I send him at any time, you can talk to him, but not a word to anyone else, understand?"

"You don't trust all your men?"

"I didn't say that. It's just a matter of being careful. Now I've got to get back to the trail post." Munson left quietly, and Hale sat on his blankets in the cold night, scratching his beard.

In the morning, as usual, Hale saw Louis astir shortly after dawn. They went down to their claims about the same time, but, by prearranged plan, they did not get together, and so it was that the spotter who had tried to watch their camps all night had little to report an hour later to Fitzpatrick.

"They didn't do nothing as far as I could tell," the man said. "Louis visited Hale's camp, like he sometimes does just before bedtime, and then he wandered back to his own fire and they went to bed."

"And so did you," Fitzpatrick said.

"No, Ewan! I kept awake, I tell you." The man held up his right hand, as if taking an oath. "I watched and I listened. . . ."

"You can't do much of either from those trees across the creek."

"I ain't getting close to that Louis's camp at night. He moves like a ghost, I tell you. One night I thought I'd sneak in a little closer, and then all at once I see him down by the creek, checking the mules . . . and I hadn't even heard or seen him leave his camp. And that mule that Hale keeps tied by his place at night. . . . Why, a mouse couldn't even. . . ."

"All right, all right," Fitzpatrick said. Maybe it was a waste of time to keep an eye on Hale and Louis, but he was still going to have the watch maintained. Their guilt or innocence would be determined just as soon as he could get some word from the traitor in Munson's bunch.

Ewan Fitzpatrick, formerly a very good sergeant of the 7th Cavalry, and, before that, a very good sergeant in the Army of the Confederate States of America, sat in the gloomy den and smiled, drumming his fingers on the table. It was a fascinating, satisfying life he was leading. He had power. With a snap of his fingers he manipulated men and events.

Men were largely fools. They lived in terror of their sorry lives. Give them a little gold, and then they lived in fear of it, also. It destroyed their power to think clearly. The man who understood those simple facts was a ruler. Aaron Bliffert's failure was that he had been a short-sighted fool. He had understood brute power well enough, but that was about the limit of his thinking. He had not understood how to play the game, to pluck the strings of men and make them give out the tune you wanted.

That was nine-tenths of the game. In the end, you took the reward, of course. Fitzpatrick smiled at the Jug on the shelf. Let them have it. Let them fight and cut each other's throats over the contents. They would do that, too, the moment his controlling hand was off them.

Poor old Aaron . . . he had been unable to grasp the fact that by giving a little, you could gain a lot. He had wanted to gather in everything at once by a head-on assault. An impatient man. A man with no zest for the game. That was why Fitzpatrick had arranged to have Giles kill him.

You had to do things like that when you were a king.

In the afternoon Peters came in from spying on the Munson guard posts. "I think they've got two men down on the trail now, sort of straddling the creek. That one up in the rocks . . . I could pick him off with one shot."

"Maybe we could pick them all off, Peters, and then we could spend a lifetime digging up the mountain to find their gold. Don't you find it easier to take it out of packs?"

Peters groaned. "That's right."

"Who's got the detail on the rock?"

"Wilson. I could see that red beard a mile away."

"Ah, yes, a fine lad, Max Wilson, and you talking of picking him off with your rifle. *Tsk, tsk!*"

The rock tower was less than 200 yards from the Southerners' cabins — a pile of broken granite where Munson's crew had made a few adjustments in the natural chaos to allow a man to sit and look between stones and survey a considerable part of the area.

It was the first time in almost a month

that Wilson had gotten duty at either the trail post or this look-out. He had been cooped up with that damned Becker and his eternal cough, and Owen Cochrane, whose enormous eyes were always watching a man with a chilly sort of look.

Wilson had plenty to resent. First off, he was the one who had found color on the branch creek. He had been getting rich, while his companions were merely digging, and then old Munson had come up with that sneaky idea about all of them going in together, to split everything they found on the whole six claims. They could do better if they all worked one claim at a time, he said.

Everyone but Wilson had voted for the plan. That was natural, they had nothing, while he had the rich claim, which he had no intention of throwing into a common pot. He had not done it, either. He had kept his own gold all the way, and it was now in a secret place. For a while the other five had not done any good at all, and then, on Bentley's claim, they had really hit it.

By then the pocket that Wilson was working had run out. He decided to throw in with the others, but they would not let him. They said he should have done it in the first place. They let him work for them all winter, but all he got was four dollars a day, while the combine was piling the stuff up like mad. Even yet he did not know how much they had taken out of the ground, but it was plenty.

His resentment had grown and grown. He felt that everyone in Spanish Creek was laughing at him. There'd been times when he'd considered joining Bliffert's bunch, but they were a little too rank to stomach. All but Fitzpatrick. You could talk to him. He understood a man's problems with a greedy bunch of friends who had cut him out of sharing a big strike.

There was just one important thing, however, that Munson and the others didn't seem to have sense enough to realize. They were not going to get out alive with their gold. But Max Wilson was. He had that solemn promise from Fitzpatrick himself.

Wilson saw a man step out from the trees below, and then step back quickly. A moment later a blue bandanna waved. By God, it was Fitzpatrick! Wilson climbed out of the rocky nest and cut across the mountain, keeping the tower between him and the cabins until he gained the trees, and then he went down to see Fitzpatrick.

"For about a month now, you haven't been on outpost duty," Fitzpatrick said.

"Does Munson suspect something?"

"Naw! How could he?"

"Then why haven't you been out?"

"Because he keeps the best shots in the cabin, excepting Becker. He can't stand it out in cold."

Fitzpatrick nodded. "Has this man Hale or the nigra been up to see you?"

"No! They're your boys, aren't they?"

"In a way, yes. They haven't been up to see you?"

"Hale stumbled in on us once. I fired a warning shot up the hill, and then Munson made him come on down. Munson questioned him a while, and then we let him go. We kept his guns."

"I see. He hasn't called on you for a talk, but has Munson gone to see him?"

Wilson shook his head. "Not that anybody knows of."

"He could have, though, couldn't he, from the trail post at night?"

"Well, I suppose so, but if he did, he sure didn't say anything about it."

"Does he talk much about his plans?"

"Sure he does!" Wilson said. "All winter long he kept blabbing about this fellow in Denver who was going to send in some men to carry out the gold. He still says they'll be here as soon as the snow goes on the passes."

"That's very interesting. How did Hale get back his guns? Did Munson take them to him?"

"No. We still got them."

"Well, I'll be blessed." Fitzpatrick clapped Wilson on the shoulder. "You're a good lad, Max, and I'm going to see that you walk out of Spanish Creek with your vast wealth, free and happy as a bird."

"It ain't no vast wealth, Mister Fitzpatrick."

"Well, whatever it may be, if I have to walk beside you, or carry you on my back, you're going to get out, and that's a guarantee from Ewan Fitzpatrick in person. And now have you discovered where the cache may be?"

"No, sir. It used to be under the floor in the east cabin, but I know they moved it after that."

"I imagine they did. Keep your ears open, Max lad. You may learn a great deal yet."

"When do I get out? A little snow won't bother. . . ."

"Soon, Max, soon. Now get back to your post and keep a sharp eye out for evil people. I hear they abound amongst these rocks and trees."

Before he left, Fitzpatrick made a narrow

study of the Munson camp and the sur-
rounding terrain. It was not the first time,
and the conclusions were about the same. It
would be no trick at all to get the guards at
the rock tower and the trail. That would
leave four men in the cabins. There was the
hard nut to crack. Oh, it could be done with
the loss of a few men, which was no consid-
eration at all.

But you still wouldn't have the gold.

It just might be that canny Munson was
trying to outwait Fitzpatrick, and, in that
case, the small war would have to be. But as
long as the passes were locked tightly, Fitzpatrick could wait. That made the game all
the better.

About dusk Louis came to Hale's fire. "It's
better than I thought. I went clear to the
top and then down far enough to make sure
of the other side. It runs right into Big
Bayou. The slow part will be getting from
Munson's camp to the trail itself. But if we
can get that far before they catch on, they'll
never overtake us. I think. . . ." Louis
stopped suddenly. "What's the matter,
Hale?"

Hale told him about Munson's insistence
on using Terrible Pass. "There must be a
good reason. I've made my guess, and now

let's see what yours is."

"I'll take the simple way," Louis said. "They've got their gold cached somewhere on the mountain close to the trail."

"That's what I think, too."

They watched the campfire for a while. Louis yawned.

"It was a long night for you," Hale said. "For nothing."

"It was not wasted time. All you have to do is make Munson change his mind about the route."

"Him? Change his mind?"

"Aren't you-all reasonable Southern gentlemen?"

"Don't start that again, Louis."

"All right, I won't. What do we do now?"

"Wait."

Louis shook his head. "Your patience is amazing. Mine has just about run out. I was even thinking of going over tonight to call on that spy they've had across the creek, but, from what I can make out, he's no longer there."

"They've decided that we're trustworthy."

"Damn," Louis said, and walked away.

Sometime after midnight, Molly warned Hale that someone was coming.

"Fatty Mitchell!" the visitor whispered, and Hale told him to come on in. He had seen Mitchell only once for a brief time. One of the things he remembered about him was a deep voice, but the whispered words did not convey any great depth of tone. Hale lit a match.

It was the right face, darkly tanned, strong, vital.

"You're worse than Munson for being careful," Mitchell grumbled. "Somebody might have seen that match."

"Either way was a chance. I'd rather be sure about you."

"We've set it for tomorrow night," Mitchell said.

"If you're still insisting on Terrible Pass, forget it."

"We'll go your way. Munson and me agreed on it."

"Just the two of you. What about the rest?"

"They'll be told at the proper time," Mitchell said. "Now here's the way Munson and me worked it out. If there's anything that you don't like, let's get it straight between us now."

At least there was some give and take in the business now, Hale thought. Mitchell laid out the plan, and Hale accepted it with the change of two minor details. The starting time was two hours later than he liked, but he knew that Munson's men had to wait until dark to bring their gold from a distant cache.

It was a simple plan. Fifteen minutes before the Southerners had all their gold at the loading point in the first gulch east of their cabins, they would send a man to Hale. Then he and Louis would go up with the mules. Munson's men would have pack saddles and panniers. Mitchell figured it would take no more than five minutes to get Hale and Louis on their way.

"What about riding saddles?" Hale asked.

"There won't be any. We'll have to use most of the straps from them to fix the pack saddles. The rats chewed hell out of things last winter."

"Bridles?"

"We'll get those patched up."

"Why hasn't it been done already?"

"We don't want to. . . . We'd rather wait," Mitchell said.

Because repairing the gear would be a dead giveaway, Hale thought. *They were going to wait until the last minute. There was someone among them they did not trust.* It was a disquieting thought.

After all the delay, the lying, the pretense, it was a great relief to Hale to know that he at last was going to make the run. There would not be much pleasure in riding a mule all the way to Denver with just a saddle blanket, but at least he would be moving, doing his job, getting the hell out of Spanish Creek.

But before he went to sleep again, he tried to think of a way to protect ownership of his claim; it would be silly to throw it away. Fate certainly had dealt him an ironic twist on that claim.

X

Hale could not keep from tensing up inside when, during his noonday meal, he saw Fitzpatrick coming. Humming a tune, swinging along unhurriedly, the man gave every appearance of being right with the world.

"Trout!" Fitzpatrick said, looking into the frying pan. "How did you do that?"

"They got trapped behind that little dam I built to keep the creek out of my test hole."

"Uhn-huh." Fitzpatrick glanced toward the claim. "I see the other day that you've been moving more dirt than usual."

"I struck it rich. That makes a difference in how you work."

Fitzpatrick laughed. "Indeed, it does!"

"I would sell it to the right man, however, but this time I want a little more than one of Giles's dollars."

267

"How much?"

"A hundred."

"Make it five hundred, and wait till the wild-eyed ribbon clerks come pouring in. They'll be starting soon."

"You really think I can get five hundred, then?"

"If anyone has it." Fitzpatrick's blue eyes twinkled. "Borrow a few pinches of gold from Allen and slip it into your pan at the right time." He started on up toward Louis's camp, and then he stopped and looked around. "I remember you had a rifle when you came, but I don't see it around any more."

"I had both a rifle and a pistol. Munson has them now, and it's none of your damned business how he got them. Until yesterday I had Louis's rifle, but I gave it back. Any more nosy questions, Fitzpatrick?"

Fitzpatrick roared with laughter. He went on up to see Louis.

Working on his claim about two hours later, Hale heard Louis talking to someone. So engrossed was he in his panning that he paid little attention to the sounds until he heard strange laughter. It sounded like a woman's voice. That simply could not be. But Hale climbed out of his shallow diggings to have a look above the willows.

He stared in wonder. It *was* a woman. The way she walked as she started back to the trail at the edge of the aspens, the shine of her dark hair in the afternoon sun. . . .

Hale started running.

"Sara!" he shouted. "Sara!"

They met a short distance below Louis's camp.

"Good Lord, Sara! How did . . . ? What are you doing here?"

"Louis was more cordial, Mister Hale." She smiled at Hale's stunned expression. "I hope you've fixed up suitable accommodations for me. Of course, I'll have to expect something a little less than the Mountain House, but. . . ."

"Suitable accommodations? Good heavens, do you realize what you've walked . . . ?" Hale looked up the valley. There was no one in sight. "Walk? How did you get here?"

Sara laughed. "I've never seen you with so little composure. Or such filthy clothing. And that beard is. . . ."

"Come on down to my camp."

"That's very generous of you."

Her heavy skirts swished and Hale's wet boots made squinching sounds as they walked. "Sara, you've got to realize that you've come into one of the toughest, dirtiest, most murderous camps in all the mountains. You surely. . . ."

"I can believe the dirty part. Is this your camp?"

"Be serious, damn it! Sit down in that chair."

"Chair?" Sara gave Hale's contrivance of aspen wood and rawhide lashing a dubious look. She sat down carefully.

Allen's men were staring. Before long the savages from the den would come streaming up the valley. "How did you get here?" Hale demanded.

"My wagons are on the other side of the pass. I had Mister Mathers select only mules that could double as pack animals. When we could go no farther with wagons, we trans-shipped to a pack train. Two of the mules didn't like that. They kept making trouble, continually slowing the train. Near the top of the pass I decided to walk on by myself. Unless those two mules got completely away, the pack train should be coming along soon."

"How many men?"

"Three. I have to keep expenses down, you know."

"You're bringing in merchandise?"

"Of course! That last night in Denver you convinced me that Spanish Creek was a veritable treasure trove . . . everyone rich,

270

and everyone probably out of supplies as a result of the long winter."

"The men here are about half starved, sure enough," Hale said darkly, "in more ways than one. You shouldn't have come. You could have saved. . . ."

"I handle my own money."

"Yeah. Any whiskey in your pack train?"

"No. I didn't think that would be wise."

"You were right there." Hale looked up the valley. "How did you get over that snow on the pass?"

"What snow? I found only a few small drifts, and they were easy to walk around."

A sudden bad feeling hit Hale. "You . . . ah . . . you didn't come over Woody Pass?"

"We didn't even consider it. Clarence Adams . . . he's my guide . . . said it would be clogged with six feet of snow, but he knew about this pass north of it, an old Indian trail."

"Oh, Christ," Hale groaned.

"What's the matter?"

"Nothing, nothing," he muttered. He saw five or six den men starting up the valley toward them. Someone down there was always on the look-out with field glasses. The sight of a woman was making the plug-uglies move faster than Hale had ever seen them go. Allen's men were coming, too. And then he saw the pack train approaching.

It quickly became a holiday occasion of shouting and bustling and more good nature than Hale had observed since his arrival in Spanish Creek. In the forefront of everything was Fitzpatrick. He put his men to work clearing out dead aspens where Sara Perkins directed that the tent be pitched; he made very sure that she could see that he was the king of Spanish Creek.

"We're a rough and ready lot in the gulch, Miss Perkins, but at heart we're as decent and respectful of womanhood as anyone you might find in a long day's journey. You have my personal guarantee that any man says or does or even looks like he wants to do anything to offend you will have to answer to me. I, Ewan Fitzpatrick, say this as judge and sheriff and leader of this district!"

About all he left out was "supreme potentate of the whole damned West", Hale thought disgustedly. Hale had his eye on Sam Mathers, Sara's right-hand man. He was tall, slender, with cold gray eyes and a tight mouth. He had merely nodded curtly when Sara introduced him.

Hale went over to where Mathers and the two packers were unloading the mules. "How was that pass you used?"

"All right." Mathers glanced toward Fitzpatrick. "How do you manage to get along with His Highness there?"

"We exist," Hale said cautiously. Ezekiel Blaine had said that he might send in decoys to help confuse the issue, and it could be that Mathers was one of them, but the man said nothing more. He walked away briskly to look at a box that one of the packers had dropped.

Hale remembered Clarence Adams — he was the ragged one who had given Hale coffee on a cold, windy day on the bank of Cherry Creek in Denver. For a while Hale thought the man did not recognize him, but then Adams grinned and said: "I thought you told me you weren't interested in mining, Mister Hale."

"I must have changed my mind."

Adams looked around the valley and shook his head. "I prospected through here two summers ago. Never got a trace of color. Now I hear it's a bigger deal than California Gulch ever was. A funny thing, mining. One time. . . ."

"Unload the packs," Mathers said. "You can mine some other time."

Louis was still on his claim, about the only man, except Munsen's group, who had not hastened to get in on the excitement. Hale went up to talk to him.

273

"Just one day more," Louis lamented. "Twelve hours would have been enough. Now what?"

"We wait, and figure something else out."

Louis nodded toward the tent that was going up. "Did any of Munson's men show up?"

Hale shook his head. "I'll have to get word to him. I'm trying to figure out how to do it without getting shot by one of their pickets."

Louis balanced his pick with the end of the handle in his palm, and then he flipped it in the air and caught it deftly. He looked at the milling crowd. The center pole of the big store tent went up, and long drapes of canvas sloped down from it. Men shouted as if they had accomplished something never done before, and Fitzpatrick yelled for them to get busy with the pegging and guying of the sides.

"Use Fitzpatrick," Louis said. "Appeal to him as high sheriff of the mountains to help you get your guns back."

"It might work." Hale started away.

"You think well of Miss Perkins, don't you?"

Hale stopped. "You know that."

"I guess we'll both be awake all night, then. There's men at the den that I wouldn't trust with a six-year-old girl."

When Hale got back to the tent, Fitz-patrick was announcing that Miss Perkins would open the store at eight the next morning. In the meantime, no one was to bother her by hanging around the place and trying to get in any advance buying. He would assign two men to guard over the tent during the night. He gave that duty to the bugler and Jordan.

"I don't think that we'll need any guard-ing, Mister Fitzpatrick, but it's very kind of you," Miss Perkins said.

"Anything, anything at all! You've brought new hope and promise to the camp of Span-ish Creek."

The flannel-mouthed son-of-a-bitch, Hale thought.

Fitzpatrick was still glowing with a fine mood when Hale got a chance to talk to him. "I want my guns back from Munson, Fitzpatrick. As sheriff, you're the man to demand that he return them."

"I'll take it under advisement."

"No. I want them now. I've waited long enough."

"You're fearful that something might hap-pen to the woman?"

"I don't trust your men any more than you do."

"Good boy!" Fitzpatrick laughed and

whacked Hale on the shoulder. "Let's go get your weapons."

When they were somewhere close to the trail post in the dark firs, Fitzpatrick shouted until he got an answer. It was Munson himself on guard. He ordered them to come in slowly. They did not see him or know exactly where he was until they were standing in a little clearing. Then Munson stepped from the trees they had already passed. "You two. I might have known. Birds of a feather. . . ."

Fitzpatrick explained why they had come.

"I don't see no reason to give them back," Munson said. "Get out of here."

Fitzpatrick raised his hand. "Legal property of my complaining friend, Munson. Now you wouldn't want to make a case before the Miners' Court, would you?"

"You'll be in hell before you two get me before that kangaroo bunch." Munson made a show of it for a few moments longer. "I'll send the guns down tomorrow."

"Sooner," Fitzpatrick said. "There's a woman with a tent full of fine supplies near Hale's camp. He wants to play at guarding her during the night."

"How did a woman get here?"

"By an open trail on a pass that, unfortunately, you never knew was there." Fitzpatrick grinned like a wolf.

Munson took it well, Hale thought. His face gave nothing away, although Hale knew that the news must have jolted him hard. "I'll send the guns down tonight. Now get out of here."

Going down the trail, Fitzpatrick chuckled. "Those high-born Southerners are a fine suspicious lot. A man might think they had a great pile of gold hidden somewhere."

"They're not guarding cotton bales."

Fitzpatrick's big laugh rolled through the trees. It grated on Hale's nerves like sand.

Fitzpatrick's orders about not hanging around the store were obeyed by the den men. Allen came over to ask all the new arrivals if they were sure they had not seen Treherne and Millerton in Denver. It was the second time he had asked, and he was almost pathetic with his inquiries. He got the same answers as before and went back across the creek more depressed than ever.

Hale got Sara aside by taking her up to see his claim. "How soon will you be out of here?"

"Does my presence upset you that much, Mister Hale?"

"By using that pass, you wrecked all my plans."

She nodded soberly then. "I think I understand. It was unfortunate for your affairs, but for me. . . ."

"You couldn't help it, but when are you leaving?"

"That depends on how fast my merchandise sells."

"You'll be rid of it in a few hours, and then I want you to get out."

"All right, I'll do that. I've still got two thousand dollars' worth of goods in the wagons, and there's another camp west of the Big Bayou that Mister Adams thinks we can reach. Being the first merchant. . . ." Sara saw Hale eyeing the mules along the creek. She read his mind. "If you're thinking of trying to involve me in your gold express. . . ."

"You could spare me one or two."

"No. I need every one of them. Mister Fitzpatrick also made his offer to buy two of them. You're dealing with a madman there."

"No, no, he's not crazy."

"He's very near to it in his own way. He gives me the chills with those eyes and that laugh of his."

"How did you find Mathers?"

"I studied him for a few days, and then I hired him. Now don't try to get him away from me. You've already stolen one man that

I wanted badly . . . Louis."

"I didn't steal him. He isn't the kind of man you can hire." Hale scowled. "Are you attracted to Mathers?"

"Do you mean am I in love with him?"

"Yes!"

"What brought that on so suddenly, Mister Hale?"

"Are you?"

"No, but it wouldn't be any of your concern if I were."

"Does he know about my business here?"

"If he does, he didn't get it from me," Sara said curtly. "Now I think we'd better go back to the camp."

Hale took her arm to assist her up the steep bank. "I wish we were together in Denver again tonight."

Her face softened and she gave him a steady look. "So do I."

She was all business after they reached the camp, conferring with Mathers about the operation of the store in the morning, and shortly afterward she retired to the small tent that had been pitched near the main one.

At dusk Peters and Jordan came up from the den. "What's that Louis doing around here?" Peters said. "We don't need him anywhere close to the woman."

"You try to go near that little tent," Hale said, "and you may find out what he's doing here."

"Huh!" Peters grinned. "How come no lantern in there? Did she have one going when she undressed?"

Mathers came up behind Peters. He turned the bugler by the shoulder and looked at him. If Hale had ever seen death in a man's eyes, it was there in Mathers's expression. Peters saw it, too. "Keep your dirty paws off me!" he said, shrugging out of the grip, but thereafter he was quiet.

Clarence Adams was full of talk about mining, and then he began to yawn in the middle of sentences. He got up from the fire and went to bed. Jordan was already dozing with his back against a tree, his rifle across his knees. After dark, Mathers drifted around as quietly as smoke, and most of the time Hale could not be sure where he was. Louis, too, was somewhere out in the dark beyond the firelight. The night was still young when Fatty Mitchell came in with Hale's weapons. He asked what time the store would open in the morning, and then he left without another word.

It wound up with Hale, Louis, and Mathers doing all the guard duty. Jordan went to sleep beside the tree, jerking and muttering as if he had bad dreams. At times he roused, shivering with cold, and went to the fire, where he sat hunched over, staring at something he saw in the flames.

Without a by-your-leave, Peters crawled into Hale's blankets in the lean-to. Dragging him out by the heels was not worth the nuisance of his sneering presence awake, so Hale let him sleep.

Cautiously Hale tried to get something out of Mathers to determine if Blaine had sent him, but the man was completely uncommunicative. It was a tense and tiresome night. Once, meeting Louis in the dark, Hale complained: "I had more rest at night during the war, most of the time."

Becker, coughing in the chill of morning, was the only one of Munson's men on hand for the opening of the store. But everyone else in Spanish Creek was there. On a folding table before the tent, Sara Perkins set up a gold scales, buying dust in even amounts, paying in greenbacks ten percent less than Denver prices. Each man was limited to $100.

Becker put up a strong argument about the limit, saying that he was representing five others, besides himself, but Fitzpatrick ruled against him. "You've heard the lady's regulations. If your friends are too lazy to appear in person, that's their hard luck."

With greenbacks in their horny paws, the miners rushed into the store where merchandise was displayed in open packs on the ground. Mathers and the two packers performed as clerks. The miners bought everything they could grab. First, the food supplies ran out — bacon slabs, canned goods, coffee beans, sugar, and flour. And then the clothing was gone — Levi's, woolen shirts, socks, hats, bandannas, and other items. Few even bothered to ask the prices. Twenty watches with steel chains and brass fobs were gone in minutes, some men buying two at $22 apiece.

Both Hale and Louis made purchases to maintain the impression that they planned to stay all summer in Spanish Creek. Becker hurried away with his stuff to send another man down from the Southerners' camp, but when Fatty Mitchell showed up, there was nothing left to buy.

Only one incident marred the turnover of the goods. Bob Giles tried to steal a pair of Levi's. Fitzpatrick caught him and made him pay double as punishment.

By the time the store was cleaned out, almost everyone had hurried away to feast and to try on new clothes. Fitzpatrick and two of his men returned before the pack train left. "We'll give you escort, Miss Perkins," Fitzpatrick said. "All that money you have might tempt some evil person."

"It's hardly a fortune, Mister Fitzpatrick."

"Ah, well, we'll go along to the top with you, just for the pleasure of the thing." Fitzpatrick looked at Hale and Louis. "And would you care to join the caravan?"

"I'll go," Louis said.

Not even counting Adams and the other packer, Sara would be safe enough as long as Mathers and Louis were with her, Hale thought, and, strange as it was, Fitzpatrick himself would be her strong protector. He fancied himself as a gallant man. Besides, all the money and dust Sara had probably did not amount to more than $1,500. For less than that, Fitzpatrick undoubtedly would send out men to waylay a fleeing miner, but he would not rob a woman. Hale still felt easier, knowing that Mathers and Louis would be with her.

The pack train left. In parting, Adams yelled back at Hale that he would return as soon as he could to stake a claim. And so would many others, too, the minute the word went out about that open pass. A week? Hale could not hope for any more time than that.

He went down to his claim. The first thing he noticed was that the creek was up. The last few days had been warm, and the high snow was beginning to go fast, but he doubted that it would go fast enough to open either Terrible or Woody within a week. Fitzpatrick would have to make a move before gold seekers came streaming in. To beat him, Hale and Louis would have to make their move first.

Fitzpatrick and Louis returned in late afternoon.

"That's a splendid little pass," Fitzpatrick said. "Too steep for wagons, but a fine trail for mules. Now isn't it a fearful shame that we all didn't know about it before?" He went on his way, laughing.

"Where are the two men?" Hale asked Louis, although he already knew.

"They went . . . hunting."

"Yeah, sure." Now the last pass was guarded. "Have you got any clever ideas?" Hale asked.

"We keep asking each other that. I haven't got any. What's yours?"

"Let's give up and shoot ourselves."

Louis glanced toward the den and smiled grimly. "No need for that. All kinds of men are just waiting to do the chore for us."

XI

Now there was no doubt that summer was coming with a rush. The creek was over its banks, flooding the placer fields, forcing the miners to move their sluices. Three times Hale had raised his dam across the beaver run to keep water out of his diggings, but he still spent a great deal of time bailing with a canvas bucket. His claim was proving even richer than before.

From the slope above the den, Bob Giles observed Hale's industrious behavior through binoculars, and then he checked to be sure that all four mules were still in the grass. The mules were the key to the whole affair. If even one of them disappeared for any length of time. . . .

Fitzpatrick sat on a stump and scratched himself luxuriously. "Don't worry about those mules, Giles. When they move, I'll know all about it."

The pack train had been gone for two days. Giles figured time to Denver. Maybe the woman did plan to go to another camp first, but you could not depend on that; the word about that easy pass would fly on the wind, and men by the hundreds would be rushing toward Spanish Creek.

"I don't like this stalling, Fitzpatrick. Our time is just about gone."

"I'll give the word on that, Giles. Hale and Louis are not the men."

"I say they are! Let's prove it one way or the other."

"And just how will we do that?"

"Simple. We'll hold a miner's meeting to vote against having niggers in the district. We'll give that Louis two days to clear out. Him and Hale being Blaine's men . . . hell, they can't be anything else . . . they'll have to make their move before the two days are up. If Louis leaves, then I'll go along with you and say that him and Hale ain't Blaine's men."

Fitzpatrick stroked his beard and yawned. The idea had an immense appeal. The truth of the matter was, he was worried himself about the inaction. Although convinced almost to the last pinch that Hale and Louis were really innocent miners, he was now wishing that they were Blaine's men, for otherwise the time was crowding hard when he would have to hit Munson's fort and run the terrible risk of never finding their gold afterward.

They would fight to the death, those Southerners; he had seen their kind do it too many times to have any doubt about it. He yawned again to mask his thoughts. It was a fine plan that Giles had suggested.

The only trouble with it was that the idea was Giles's and not Ewan Fitzpatrick's.

"Your idea is no good whatsoever," Fitzpatrick said, "and I'll have no arguments to the contrary. Now give me those glasses and go down and see who has his greedy eye on the Jug."

If Fitzpatrick and Giles had their problems, Hale and Louis were walking an even keener edge of doubt and worry. There were three men now on the open pass, camped, and one still left on Woody. Mitchell said the guards on Terrible Pass could be handled, but neither he nor Munson had any solution for the snow. And Munson was like a rock in his determination that the gold had to go out.

He had a point that Hale could not deny. If the gold did not move, Fitzpatrick would make his blow against the cabins and never quit until all resistance was crushed. His only hope would be to get one man alive, and that would have to be either Munson or Mitchell, because Munson had at last admitted in a nocturnal conference that only he and Mitchell knew where the cache was, close to the trail on Terrible Pass.

"They won't get either one of us alive," Munson said. "I'll guarantee that."

Another point that he now revealed was

that the Southerners had very little ammunition. "I know I told you we could hold out for days, but it wasn't so."

"If Louis and I get away with the gold, they'll come in on you, anyway, just for revenge," Hale said.

"Probably. A few might do that. But with the gold gone and them knowing it, attacking us wouldn't have much meaning to them. I ain't worrying about that, Hale. You just get the gold out and we'll take care of everything else."

Hale had already talked to Ed Allen about having his men join Munson's group for common defense at the fort. It could be done swiftly in the daytime, and Allen's men could take their gold with them, and then the combined force could hold out easily until the valley was full of men. Allen said that offer had been turned down once before by the Southerners, but that he was willing to talk it over again with his group.

But Munson would not have any part of it, after Hale suggested the idea. "Those Allen blue-bellies! To hell with that! Allen was with a battery that killed kin of mine at Chickamauga and some of those others with him wrecked my company at Sharpsburg. That Holmes was with Sherman in Georgia, and. . . ."

"All right, all right, take it easy."

"Keep your Yankee friends, Hale. We haven't had any trouble with Allen's gang, but I don't need them. Let them run for help somewhere else. You just get that gold out for us and everything will be fine."

It would be very fine, indeed, Hale thought sourly, if he had any idea of how to achieve the impossible. "I may have something worked out by tomorrow night."

"You'd better," Munson said. "The time is on us. I'll send Mitchell tomorrow night. You can trust him."

He had made that last remark several times. It confirmed Hale's belief that Munson had friends who could not be trusted.

"Tomorrow night" was now only about two hours away, and neither Hale nor Louis had any plan to give to Mitchell. They sat by Hale's fire and mulled things over. The river was still rising, washing back into the willows, making a steady pounding sound.

"I'm desperate enough to build a birch-bark canoe and run out on the creek," Hale said.

"Chop and burn it out of a log. The problem is, we'd capsize, gold and all, before we got as far as the den."

"Big cañon on the west end of the valley, eh?"

Louis nodded. "That's what Clarence Adams said. At low water, he said, he couldn't even walk through it, let alone take his mule."

The statement turned a key in Hale's mind. "I think you've struck the answer, Louis!"

"Log canoe? You're crazy."

"I mean, walk. That's the answer! All we've ever thought about is how to get out with the mules packing that gold. Forget the mules. The instant we start anywhere with them, we're in trouble."

"Pack it out on our backs." Louis's eyes began to gleam.

"Any time after dark we can make our start, and. . . ."

"No. We'll start in the daytime, right after breakfast. They won't expect that. We'll have a good chance of getting a full eight hours or more ahead of them before they realize what we're up to."

"It'll work! By Tophet, it'll work!"

They built the plan up as the only feasible solution to their problem. The daylight start, the mules left where they always foraged, the fact that no one in his right mind would think a man would tackle a snowy pass with at least eighty pounds of gold on his back. It was simple. It looked good. But then they tore the plan apart, and the separate pieces did not look so good. Leaving the mules behind might not fool Fitzpatrick in the least. He did not know that they had to backpack eighty pounds apiece. For all he knew, that could be the total. Maybe he expected them to make a run on foot, and was waiting for them to try it. Eighty pounds was a sum that fell easily enough from the lips, but at high altitude it was a weight that could burn the lungs right out of a man trying to hurry. And there was the snow. There was no choice of passes; they had to go by Terrible because it was the only way that would take them with relative quickness to where they could get animals for the rest of the trip to Denver.

Even if they could get past the guards on the pass north of Woody, they would have fifty miles of open country to cross on foot. Terrible Pass it had to be, the route that Hale had hoped he would never see again. "The more we study this thing, the worse it's going to look," he said. "The question is, do we try it or not?"

"We have to do it," Louis said quietly. "It's all we have. Now, what about the mules after Fitzpatrick knows we're gone?"

"That's worried me, too. They'll use them to go after us, so the only thing that's left is to have Allen cut their throats as soon as he sees a big stir around the den."

Louis shook his head. "That means you'll have to tell him we're going. I think you can trust him, but what happens to him when Fitzpatrick sees what he's done?"

"Yeah." Hale frowned. "Then someone from Munson's camp will have to do it."

Louis's face was the picture of gloom. "That's the only part I don't like."

"I'll see that Blaine pays for them."

"You think that'll make it all right?"

"What else is there to do but kill them?"

Louis nodded. "All right, but just don't talk about it any more."

Allen came over shortly afterward to ask what Munson's reaction had been to a joining of forces. "Our bunch is just about ready to do it."

"He thinks he can hold out with the men he has," Hale said.

Allen made a sighing sound. "You know, if we had ever gotten around to burying the god-damned war, we could have gone together and walked out of this place. I don't know what happened to our brains and guts during the winter."

"They turned to gold," Louis said.

Hale took the step. He told Allen what he and Louis had in mind, and he asked him about killing the mules.

"All right," Allen said. "I'll do it, but not with a knife."

"We haven't agreed on it with Munson yet," Hale said. "He might turn the whole idea down. In that case, we won't be going, so, after breakfast, I'll hang my frying pan right there on that tree where you can see it from the creek. If you don't see it, and we're not around, you'll know we've gone. Then it will be up to you to keep your eye on the den.

"We hope we'll have all day, but, if something goes wrong and they catch on, you'll see some excitement around the den. That will be the time for you to do your job. Not too soon, you understand. Don't do it until you're sure they're on to us, and, for God's sake, not too late."

"I understand." Allen's gaze was steady. He did not like it and he was afraid of getting involved, but he would do his part.

When Mitchell came that night, he, too, found a lot in the plan that he did not like. "Did you ever carry eighty pounds on your back at twelve thousand feet, on the run?" he asked.

"No," Hale said.

"Let me tell you why our gold is where it is. Munson and I started out with it last winter, on snowshoes. There was a damned sight less of it than there is now. By the time we got to the trail, we knew we couldn't make it. Maybe I could have. I don't know. But Munson would never have made it across the pass. We had intended to move our cache, anyway, so we hid it up there on the mountain and came back. Since then we've added most of what we mined afterward. It's all up there, and it's one hell of a weight for two men. You're sure you can't work the mules into it some way?"

"No, we can't," Hale said.

"Snowshoes are one thing," Louis said. "Men on dry ground are something else. We'll make it."

"Dry ground?" Mitchell said. "Up there?"

"We won't use the trail until near the top," Louis said.

"You still can't dodge all the snow, especially in the timber." Mitchell fell silent, thinking about it.

"Well?" Hale asked after a time.

Mitchell nodded. "It's the only chance there is, but I'll have to go back and talk it over with Munson before I can say yes or no. Have you got two strong packs?"

"One, so far," Louis said. "We'll get the other tonight from Allen."

"We'll bring them if we decide to try it,"

Mitchell said. "If it's no, I'll come back and tell you. If it's yes, meet us tomorrow in the timber west of the rock tower. You know where that is?"

"Where you keep the look-out?" Louis asked.

"That's it. Be there at eight."

"I'd rather start an hour earlier than that," Hale said.

"It has to be eight. That's when we change the guard, and I don't want. . . . Eight o'clock."

Hale spent a restless night. Every time he woke, he could see Molly standing where he had tied her. She had been an excellent watchdog, but for the rest of the night she had no cause to give the alarm.

Mitchell did not return.

After breakfast, Hale left his frying pan beside the fire. Both he and Louis went to their claims, Hale leading Molly up with the other mules. He waved his hand at Louis — the signal that the deal was on. It was a little before six by the watch Hale had bought in the tent store. They had about an hour to kill before starting.

Watching the den, Hale made a show of working. He saw the sun glint on binoculars and knew that the observation post was working as usual. Allen's men went to work about ten minutes later. They had moved one sluice back from the flooding creek, and now they were shifting the second one. And then Hale saw Allen coming toward him.

"I got mixed up," Allen said. "The frying pan . . . I couldn't remember whether. . . ."

"We're going." Hale gave his pick to Allen for the benefit of the man with the field glasses.

"I'm sorry," the man said. "A simple little thing like whether the pan was on the tree, or not. . . . I guess I'm nervous this morning." He went back to his group.

Hale made the first move. He walked slowly back to his camp, limping. He built the fire up, and then he went back into the trees and waited. Not long afterward Louis went to the mules and pretended to be checking their picket ropes, and then he went on to his camp unhurriedly.

An hour later Fred Huber, the watcher with the field glasses, caught just a glimpse of Hale shaking out a blanket and tossing it on a bush to air in the sun. But it was not Hale; it was Ethan Holmes, sent by Allen on a long detour up the valley and through the trees, after crossing to the north side of the creek, to make just a flash appearance at the camp.

It completely fooled Huber. He reported a little later to Fitzpatrick that Hale and Louis had quit work because of high water and were loafing in their camps.

And that was just about the same time that Louis and Hale and Munson and Mitchell stopped beside a slushy snow bank in the trees below the Terrible Pass trail to confer about the first bad obstacle.

Munson pointed a bony finger and spoke softly. "About two hundred yards up there. If you hear a gunshot, forget the whole thing and get back to your camps."

"We'll be back in a half hour," Mitchell said grimly.

It had become a lazy routine for the two men guarding the trail in the daytime. In a little rocky cove where the trail made a turn, they were out of the chill wind off the melting snow and the sun was warm on them. Even while sitting, by leaning forward they could see parts of the trail below them and a good deal of the valley. Any mule that came up the trail would make noise enough to be heard for a mile in the clear, thin air.

Perrault was stretched out in sleep. With his back against a rock, Clarkson was dozing, his rifle leaning against a rock beside him.

The stone dislodged from above roused Clarkson with a start, but he never really got into full action. He had his hand on his rifle when Fatty Mitchell came down on him with a five-pound rock in his hand. Clarkson had one leg under him, trying to rise. Mitchell swung the rock against his head with fearful force, and Clarkson's dreams of gold were gone forever. So forceful was the blow that Mitchell was carried right on through by it, off balance. He fell across Clarkson's body, and the rock got away from him.

Although he had been asleep, Perrault came out of it like an animal. He leaped up and almost had the pistol out of his belt when Munson came over the edge of the rocky trail like a gaunt, leaping wolf. Perrault never saw him. The knife in Munson's hand went in and up as his bony wrist flashed across Perrault's shoulder and slammed into his throat.

Mitchell rose, favoring one leg. Like Munson, he was in his stocking feet.

"Get the guns and all their shells," Munson said.

In less than Mitchell's promised half hour they were back with Louis and Hale, who asked no questions. Munson paused only to wash his hands in the snow. "Come on."

The cache was in the needle mat under a clump of spruce trees. Mitchell and Munson put poke after poke into the packs they had supplied. Munson tossed aside a coiled rope Louis had brought. "That could be the straw that broke the camel's back."

"I'll tote it just the same," Louis said. "We might have to go down a cliff or something."

The gold all stowed, Mitchell and Munson exchanged packs and hefted them. They agreed that the weights were about even. When Mitchell helped him into the pack, Hale knew he had never carried such a concentration of weight before. He knew it would get heavier. As a parting remark he said: "You ought to consider throwing in with Allen."

Munson pointed up the mountain.

As the two men began to climb, Mitchell kept rubbing his right hand on his pants leg. "That Clarkson wasn't too bad a sort. I remember last fall. . . ."

"Only a murderer," Munson said. "That rifle you've got belonged to Jake Woolf. You remember when he started out of here last fall?"

With a startled expression Mitchell grabbed up the weapon and studied it. "You're right," he said grimly. "It is Jake's rifle."

Munson kept looking up the mountain. "If we don't hear that god-damned Yankee bugle in the next four hours, I'll give them a good chance to make it, even if Allen botches his job on the mules. If they don't make it, Blaine still pays eighty percent."

Mitchell was absorbed with the rifle. "I feel better about Clarkson, seeing this."

"You're a fool, if you feel bad about any of those dirty sons-of-bitches. Don't think we won't have to spread a few more of them out on the rocks before this thing is over."

They hurried back toward the three-cabin fort. It was the first time since they had moved their cache up on the mountain that they had both been away at the same time from the cabin. And that was a fact that was worrying both of them.

XII

Red-headed Max Wilson and Becker held the west cabin — Becker in his bunk and Wilson moving restlessly from one loophole to another. From the gun slot in the end wall, Wilson had seen Mitchell go to the rock post, but he had not stayed there more than a few minutes. Munson was supposed to be at the trail post.

The night before, Munson had relieved Mitchell at the trail post. That was strange, because for some time the two of them had never been away together. They had been gone for more than an hour during the night, and now they had been away for more than two hours.

"Why don't you stop jumping around like bacon in a frying pan?" Becker growled.

"Why don't you stop coughing?" Wilson went back to the end loophole. If Hale and that Louis were really the men from Blaine and were trying something, and, if he missed giving the warning, Fitzpatrick would not have much mercy on him.

Then Wilson saw them coming on the run, out of the trees, across the open space below the tower. He could truthfully say that he did not recognize them for sure — that is, for a short time. And then he knew that it was Mitchell and Munson. His suspicions snapped together and made a fact: the move was on. He fired three shots, well off to one side of the running men.

Becker leaped from his bunk and ran to a loophole.

A moment later Bentley came rushing in from the middle cabin. "What is it?"

Wilson was trying to fan away the heavy black powder smoke as he peered through the slot. "My God! I think I made a mistake. It looks like . . . it looks like. . . ."

Bentley shoved him away from the loop-hole and peered out. "You damned fool, that's Fatty and Steve up there!"

"I couldn't tell for sure. Anyway, I just fired a warning."

The stinking fumes drove Becker outside, coughing worse than ever. Owen Cochrane came to the doorway of the middle cabin. "What happened?"

Becker shook his head disgustedly. When he stopped coughing, he said: "Wilson got excited."

A moment later the thin notes of a bugle sounding "Charge!" carried up from the den. For a long moment Becker's pale, wasted face wore the tortured expression of one who refuses to believe the terrible truth.

With his pistol hanging at full arm's length beside his leg, he walked back into the cabin, stared at Wilson for an instant, and then shot him in the chest.

The Allen men heard the three shots and began to argue about the source. Then the bugle made its strident notes. "Back to the cabins, men," Allen said. Something had turned in him; he was still afraid, but no longer afraid to act. He drew his pistol and plunged into the creek. Near the far bank he slipped on the smooth stones and fell full-length. He staggered to his feet and ran toward the mules, slowing when he got close, in order not to spook them. At close range he took deliberate aim at Molly's head. The cap on the nipple misfired.

Wet from the creek, all the caps failed. He had no others closer than the camp, and now it was much too late for a trip there and back. They had seen him from the den, and three men were running up the trail. Since he had nothing but a pocket knife, the best he could do was free the mules. Two of the ropes were attached by means of harness snaps, and two were hard-tied knots. It was quicker to unbuckle the halters and slip them off than to fool with the knots. He yelled and swung a picket rope, and the mules trotted up the valley.

He crossed the creek on another plunging run and scrambled toward the trees. Two shots came close to him before he gained cover and sprinted toward the cabins. All the way he was cursing himself for being a clumsy, careless idiot who had helped wreck Louis and Hale's chances by falling down in the creek. The only consolation he had was that he had at last thrown off crippling fear, enough to do his best to carry out a promise.

■ ■ ■ ■

On the mountain, Louis kept warning Hale to slow down lest he burn himself out before they were well started. To avoid the snow, they crossed the trail and stayed in the rocks as much as possible. There was a long, bare rib that they could have followed for a long distance, but it would have exposed them to a keen-eyed watcher in the valley, and so they stayed below the rib in the tumbled rocks.

They had not gone far before they heard the rocking sounds of three rifle shots. And then the bugle call.

"We're in for it now," Louis said calmly.

"So soon? How did they catch on so fast?"

"The devil has his ways." Louis climbed on a rock to study the mountain ahead. "We won't get over today."

"Why not?"

"They can beat us to the top. If we lose our heads and try to make a race of it now, we'll lose."

After he thought about it for a few moments, Hale had to agree. They had only begun the climb, and the weight of his burden was already asserting itself. The higher they went, the heavier it would become. He had no intention, however, of huddling under a rock like a rabbit and waiting for some miraculous stroke of luck to take care of him.

"I'd say our best chance is to keep going up slowly, sticking to the rocky parts," Louis said. "Let's get as close to the top as we can, and then. . . . We'll just have to see how things look after that."

Anything was better than sitting still, Hale thought.

Pursuit of Louis and Hale was by no means instant, for the simple reason that Fitzpatrick was not sure that they had gone anywhere very far from camp. He had Wilson's three-shot signal, to be sure, but all that told him was that Wilson thought some move was under way to take out the Southerners' gold.

He sent three men to get the mules, and, when Allen turned them loose and spooked them up the valley, that certainly appeared to be confirmation of the belief that Louis and Hale were afoot somewhere with gold on their backs. Fitzpatrick did not know how much gold that might be, but he was sure that it would be a considerable weight. Wilson's last guess had been 200 pounds, probably an inflated estimate, but make it one 150 — that was still a fearful burden for two men to get away with on foot.

Fitzpatrick sat down on a stump in front of the den and made an appraisal of the situation. His men were jumping-eager to start pursuit in some direction — any direction — and some of them were muttering that the waiting had been a bad mistake.

Fitzpatrick got up on the stump and bellowed for silence. "I'm not even sure that anything's happened. It may be a trick to start us running in circles. The passes are all guarded, so how far do you think anyone is going to get? Now here's my orders. . . ."

He sent men to reinforce the guards on the two passes up the valley. He ordered Peters and Jordan to go to the top of Terrible Pass as fast as they could, taking the two guards on the trail with them. He sent one man down the river to check for tracks near the big cañon. It was a highly unlikely escape route, since it led deeper into the mountains, but Fitzpatrick could not overlook it. Only limping, Walt could stay and keep his eye on the Jug.

There was one important fact that Giles had missed, and now it colored his thinking. It was he who had been on duty with the field glasses when the gunshots came. Trying to see too many things at once, he had missed the fact that Allen had tried to shoot the mules.

"They've gone toward the dry pass," Giles said. "That's why Allen stampeded the mules in that direction."

"Maybe," Fitzpatrick said.

"Sure. They went that way."

"Fifty miles of open country in Big Bayou?"

"If they catch a couple of those mules. . . ."

"Our boys are smack in the middle of that pass. They'll do the mule-catching if anybody does it."

"They found out something about this country from that Adams that we don't know, I tell you! Big Bayou is just the route no man would try on foot, and that's just why they did it . . . to fool us," Giles insisted.

"Maybe. What about Terrible Pass?"

Giles cursed. "You'd have to be an idiot to try to make a fast trip over that. In the first place, to get past the guards, they'd have to go up one of those gorges. That would take a mountain goat all day."

"Maybe."

"What do you know that you ain't told me?" Giles asked suspiciously.

"I know that the short way out is over Terrible Pass, and, if I thought I had four, five hours' start on somebody that was going to chase me, that's the way I'd head."

Having made his decision, Fitzpatrick went into the cabin and began to throw a pack together. "When someone gets back here with a mule, Giles, tell them to bring it up to me on Terrible Pass."

"Oh, no, Ewan boy! I'm going with you. Walt can tell them."

Fitzpatrick shrugged. "Suit yourself." He set such a fast pace up the first quarter mile of trail that both he and Giles were gasping.

"It won't work," Giles panted. "I always did have better lungs than you. Go your best. I'll be right at your heels."

"Now why would I try to run away from you on such a fine morning, with all the beautiful scenery around us?"

Giles saved his breath.

They came to the dead guards. "Would you look at that?" Fitzpatrick said without the least trace of emotion. "Ah, well, it makes a little more in the Jug for the boys."

There were no tracks through the first long snow bank. Dislodged rocks and dirt on the surface close to the bank showed that someone had climbed around it. "We may as well get used to it right here," Fitzpatrick mused. "So our two rabbits don't like our fine trail."

The tracks of two men were all they ever saw as they climbed on up. Where forced to it by the terrain, Peters and Jordan had gone through the snow banks, but they had avoided them where they could.

Although he had slowed the pace to a crawl, with frequent stops to rest, Fitzpatrick was gray in the face and his hands were trembling when they sat down on a rock a half mile from the top. From where they sat, the rest of the way looked clear.

"Did it ever occur to you that killing Perrault and Clarkson was all a part of a feint to draw us up here?" Giles asked. "Some of Munson's men did that, while Hale and Louis headed for the dry pass."

"Maybe."

They heard the clatter of rocks on the trail high above. Giles used the field glasses. "That's Peters coming back. They didn't come this way, Fitzpatrick!"

"Not all the way over, but they're somewhere on the mountain."

Giles cursed. "How do you know? After they heard that bugle, they probably ran back to Munson's camp. I tell you, we waited too long."

"Go find them at Munson's camp, if you think that's where they are."

Giles kept eyeing him narrowly while they waited for Peters to come down and report.

"No sign of them," Peters said. "What do

we do now?"

"Get ready for a long wait and a cold night," Fitzpatrick said cheerfully. "Where's Jordan?"

"On top. He's got a pain in his arm. Says it's his heart."

"Too bad," Fitzpatrick said. "Here's what we'll do. . . ." He had been studying the mountain. Only crazy men would try to cross the spine. Hale and Louis would have to go through the slot.

Three more of Fitzpatrick's men arrived shortly before the sound of rifle fire came up from the valley. The three had chased the mules, but, led by a wicked brown one, the animals had kept doubling around in the timber like deer. The mule chasers were coming back from their futile pursuit when some of the guards from the eastern passes had caught up with them.

The guards had decided that the whole thing was a ruse to confuse them. Hale and Louis had gone to the Rebels' cabins to help them hold out, and there was where the gold was, also. The thing to do was to go get it.

Fitzpatrick considered the noise of the firing. First, it had been a quick outburst, full of determination and fury. Then his men had learned how tough the place was, and they had settled down to a siege. The damned fools.

Every shot would bring more stragglers in from outpost duty. They would all scramble to get in on loot that wasn't even there. He knew his men well. There would be other little complications, too, but what went on below no longer mattered to Ewan Fitzpatrick.

What Fitzpatrick did not know was that Ed Allen had gotten himself untracked to the full extent. He was no longer asking for votes, but giving orders. Soon after retiring to the cabins, he had sent one man up a tree to observe the den. He already knew some of Fitzpatrick's dispositions of his gang, and it was no trick to count as his observer reported men leaving in various directions.

It did not prove easy to shake loose the fear and habit that had grown like winter moss in the camp, but Allen was a driver now. "Take your damned gold and all the grub we've got. We're going to join the Rebs, whether they want us or not."

Moving was simple, once they started. Allen and two others even took time to take the food in Hale's and Louis's camps. Getting in with the Southerners was the hardest part of the move. They had pulled their outposts in and were edgy. Cochrane put a bullet into the tree that Allen stood behind while waving a dirty undershirt on a stick; it was the nearest thing to white he had.

Even after they established his identity, the Southerners took their time. Mitchell and Munson argued the thing over fiercely, before Mitchell at last prevailed and got the Civil War in abeyance, if not forgotten. The joining was effected, and Munson, eyeing the bulging food packs, growled: "You Yankee bastards always did have more grub than us."

Allen was not through yet. He placed four good shots in the rocks above the cabin. When the attack came, those four let the fort answer, until, from their vantage points on high ground, they spotted good targets. The quartet earned their keep. They killed two den men and wounded a third, and then, under the covering fire of the defenders, they ran downhill and joined their companions.

Leopold Schmidt had taken charge of the attack, and now he began to grasp its magnitude. He had some doubts, but he hung on with the few men he had, and later he was reinforced by the guards who had abandoned the passes to the east.

Average plunderers might have given up, but these men had seen gold poured into the Jug too many times to doubt that both Allen's men and the Rebels had a vast amount of it inside the cabins. Schmidt convinced them that Hale and Louis had only faked a run with the Southerners' wealth.

"Just before dawn we'll pick them off like rats running out of a burning straw pile."

In the den itself, Walt had been ready for a long time. He grunted under the weight of the Jug as he hobbled out to a crevice he had picked in the rocks behind the cabin. With an axe he cut through both layers of flinty leather and poured the contents into the crevice, and then he sealed it with the same plug of rotting leaves that he had lifted from the crevice. He blew away the last few yellow specks on the rock, wiped his tracks out with a spruce bough, drove the axe back into the chopping block, and put the Jug back on its shelf, the cut part toward the corner.

He had seen Allen's men abandon their camp, and he had counted his own companions as they came down the valley and went up the branch creek to join the siege. They were fools; they never would get into those cabins, and they had left that dry pass wide open.

Walt rolled his blankets on the table for over-the-shoulder carrying. He began to fill a pack with food. Even if he had to hide out somewhere around the edge of Big Bayou for a month or more, it would be worth it when he came back.

He tensed when he heard the thump of feet outside. And then Joseph Undset came in. He was the one Fitzpatrick had sent down the river. "Not a damned track down that way," Undset said. "We're hitting old Munson's camp, huh?"

"Yeah. We'd better get on over and give a hand."

Undset had grown used to the dim light. Suddenly he grabbed the pack and dumped it. The only gold dust that fell out was in Walt's poke. Scowling, Undset walked over to the Jug and lifted it. "Walt, you dirty, thieving. . . ."

Undset staggered back as the first bullet from Walt's rifle hit him in the stomach. Walt fired again, aiming carefully. And then he gathered up his scattered food supplies and limped away up the valley. He saw no one. They were still firing more or less steadily up at Munson's camp.

■ ■ ■ ■

At dusk the three men Fitzpatrick had detailed to stay on the south side of Terrible Pass, close to where they had caught up with him and Giles, decided that Fitzpatrick had made a big mistake. All the action was down at Munson's place. Hell, Hale and Louis would have been crazy to have made a run with gold up this lung-busting mountain. The three took off as fast as they could; they had no intention of being left out of the division of spoils.

In the reeking, choking powder fumes of the middle cabin, Allen was making more plans. Before dawn he was going to sneak six men out and get them into position for a flank assault against the men going down in the trees. "We're going to get those murdering bastards," he said. "We'll drive what's left back to their own cabin, and then burn it around their ears."

Munson was convinced that Allen would do just about what he said, but he did not go as far as telling the damned Yankee what he thought.

Two men deserted Schmidt during the night. They sneaked back to the den and found Joseph Undset dead beside the empty

Jug. The Jug had been their talisman, their symbol of success, with a promise of greater success when they split the Southerners' gold. Now the Jug had been rifled and the Rebels' gold was in a fort that could not be taken. Fitzpatrick had run out. Things were coming apart too fast. The two men got their possessions together and headed up the valley.

On the dry pass trail at dusk, Walt heard riders coming behind him. He began a limping run that quickly wore him out. Panting with fear and near exhaustion, he swung his rifle around and waited. There were no riders on the two mules coming up the trail. Walt walked back toward them slowly. The one in front had a halter.

"Easy now, steady," Walt coaxed.

The animals stood stockstill until he was quite close. He made a grab for the halter as the first mule suddenly lunged ahead. The mule jerked its head high, and its shoulder struck the man and sent him spinning off the narrow trail to break his neck in the rocks below.

Darkness came and the firing stopped at the cabins on the branch creek.

XIII

Gold was not worth it . . . not even life itself was worth it, Hale told himself savagely. It had been the most terrible exertion of his life, and then the bitter night among the rocks was enough to make a man doubt his sanity. Neither he nor Louis was sure of where they were, and now, shortly before dawn, Louis had been gone for almost an hour.

Thin, gray light began to appear on the crest above Hale. Stiff and chilled, he looked up at the plunging heights and vowed to bend his rifle over Louis's head, if Louis even suggested going up there.

He heard a light clattering of rocks that announced Louis's return. At the same time, the distant thump of rifle fire came up from the valley. For a short time it was almost a solid roll of sound. Then, with a few scattered shots, it ended.

Hale did not know it, of course, but Allen had taken not six but ten men in on the flank of the besiegers and had shattered them and sent them in flight.

Louis came on over to Hale. "We're east of the pass and higher than it. I think there's one man right above the narrow part, but I can't be sure yet."

Hale took one more look at the crest.

"Yes," Louis confirmed. "The pass is the only way."

From the concealment of rocks 200 yards from the pass, they studied the guard sitting above the slot. The light kept growing. "He's asleep," Louis whispered.

They dropped down the mountain and crept in closer. It was now an easy rifle shot. Careful not to scrape steel on rock, Louis sighted on the guard.

"Wait a minute." Hale frowned, staring from between two rocks. "I think that man is already dead." It came from old war scenes, repeated over and over. "Keep your rifle on him while I go in."

He went all the way, climbing far enough above the slot to be sure. It was the one called Jordan. Hale saw no marks of violence, but the man was dead, propped up in the rocks as a target to draw a shot to warn the others.

Louis was scrambling toward the slot, his pack on his back, with Hale's pack on his shoulder. He was gasping from exertion. He lay down full-length to rest, and, when he caught his breath, he said: "Gold makes an uneasy pillow, Brother Hale."

They crawled ahead slowly, until they could peer over the north side of the pass. The immediate trail went down by switchbacks in steep drops, and then between two soaring heights of granite it crossed the wide, nearly level place that Hale had wondered about when he and Louis walked it in a driving snowstorm. Piles of rocks, the cairns, marked the route to where it turned through a narrow break in the granite. That was the place, Hale recalled, that he had thought was the top of the pass.

"Man behind that second cabin, flat on his belly," Louis said suddenly.

"I don't see him."

"I don't either now, but a leg or something moved."

There were six cairns. They scooted back to where they could stand unseen.

"Got this one figured out?" Louis asked.

"They may not take a chance on long shooting if we go down like we didn't suspect a thing. As soon as we reach the flat, you go right and I'll go left. We'll get the angle on them. Run and sprawl, Louis, run and sprawl. Take cover where you can find it, but keep moving in."

They went down the trail as if they owned the mountain. It worked. No shots came until after they started running in opposite directions. The first belly flop Hale took, the weight of his pack made it seem that he had broken all his back ribs.

The powder smoke was at the second and the fourth cairns. On his next dive Hale came down short of cover. He heard a bullet rip into the pack. That gave him energy to scrabble forward until he hit a small depression. He had not counted shots, but he judged from the smoke that the man behind the second pile of stones was doing most of the firing. Three more gut-twisting, lung-busting sprints, and Hale was out far enough to get the angle. After he got his breath where he lay in a bank of dirty snow, he crawled on to get behind a rock. He wasn't sure that he could see the man's legs, but he sighted slowly and put a shot just behind the second cairn.

That brought quick reaction. The bullet was close enough to make the man shift position. And now he was exposed to Louis's fire. All the while, the man at the fourth cairn was firing deliberately. He splashed one bullet on Hale's rock, but for the most part he was wild because of the great range.

Hale and Louis concentrated on the first man. They were the end points of the base of a wide, squat triangle, and their target was the apex. No matter which way the man twisted, his legs were targets for one of them. They made it so hot for him that he leaped up to run. And that was when they got him. His hat flew off as he fell, and Hale saw blond hair, and he thought it was Peters, the bugler.

With alternate rushes, and sometimes lunging ahead simultaneously, they moved in on the second man. First one and then the other fired at him. He did not break. They got him in the legs, but he continued to shoot until a ricochet from the stone smashed into his brain. That one was Giles.

They looked down on him briefly after they converged. "He beat me with a whip," Hale said.

"He lashed my people for a thousand years," Louis said. "Him and all his kind."

Beyond the gap ahead, around the rocky point where the ledge of a trail gave no possibility of flanking, they knew there must be others waiting. They walked on slowly, their packs an intolerable weight. Now and then they looked back to see if there was pursuit. Before they reached the gap, Louis said: "Wait a minute!"

A mule was coming briskly down the pass. It paused and then made a wide detour around the second cairn and again when it approached Giles's body.

"That's Molly!" Hale said.

"Let's go."

They hurried now until they blocked the gap. Molly kept coming toward them, eyeing them, hesitating. Hale took off his pack and walked toward her. She retreated. He turned away and she followed. Each time he moved toward her, it was the same thing all over again. Mustering patience that he had not known he had, Hale kept at it, until at last Molly walked up to him and let him seize her halter. He led her up to Louis, who had already cut a piece from his rope and was lashing the shoulder straps of the packs together. Hale grabbed the rest of the rope and tied one end to her halter.

"You hold on," Louis said. "I'll sling the packs." He grunted with the effort of lifting the packs across the mule's back. The weight settled. Molly looked around inquiringly, and then she tried to bolt.

It took both of them to hold her. Suddenly she was docile again, but they both knew that if she ever got away, they would not see her again until they reached Silver Bell. They put Molly in the lead. Walking behind her, they carried their rifles in one hand and clung to the rope with the other.

She gave the warning sooner than they had expected. On the third sharp turn beyond the narrows, she stopped suddenly, stamping her hoofs, her ears pricked forward. It was cliff on one side and wall on the other, and someone was waiting around the turn. They put their rifles down and drew their pistols.

The mule had the trail blocked. For a moment Hale thought of going over her, and then he considered crawling between her legs to get ahead. Both ideas were short-lived. Molly was already nervous.

They heard a familiar laugh. "Now that was a sneaky trick, boys, to put that brown mule in the lead in order to sniff out an honest man like myself. But since it's the only trail off the mountain, I'll forgive you. Come right ahead and we'll all walk down together like the old friends that we are."

Receiving no answer, Fitzpatrick laughed again. "Hale? Louis? Don't be bashful. No use to play 'possum like that. I saw you come down the pass, and I saw the terrible patty-cake you played with my lads behind the stones, and I even saw you catch the mule."

Hale was looking over the edge. The view of jagged rocks about 100 feet below was enough to turn his stomach. He had to steel himself to keep from looking all the way to the bottom. He had to concentrate on the narrow ledge about eight feet below. Then he pointed to himself and shook his head violently at Louis. He sat down and began to remove his boots.

"Have you boys figured out something yet?" Fitzpatrick called. He was in high good humor.

"We buried the gold," Louis said. "That was nothing but rocks you saw us put on the mule."

"I believe you. Come right along."

"What's your proposition, Fitzpatrick?" Louis asked.

"Hale? Has the cat got your tongue?"

"He's back in the narrows, waiting for some of your men to show up," Louis explained.

Hale slipped over the edge. He had a bad moment before his feet touched the ledge. With his arms spread wide, he began to work his way along the face of the cliff. There was only a light breeze, but it put a cold touch on the sweat that seemed to have broken out suddenly all over him.

Louis kept Fitzpatrick talking, and Hale judged the distance he had to go by the sound of the man's voice. He continued to inch along the trail until he knew he was quite close to Fitzpatrick. He got his left foot into a toehold about two feet above the ledge. He eased his pistol out. Suddenly there was no conversation on the trail. Louis had said something a few moments before, but now Fitzpatrick was silent.

Hale lived another long, tense moment before he heard Fitzpatrick say: "I can stay here a long time, Louis. How long can you keep that nervous mule from running?"

Hale went up, driving off the toehold, clutching with his left hand. He got his head and shoulders above the trail. Fitzpatrick was about ten feet away, pressed back into a niche in the rocks. His rifle was covering the turn, and he was grinning as he talked.

It was not intentional, but the first shot slammed into the rifle and knocked it from Fitzpatrick's hands. He had his pistol half drawn when Hale's second bullet hit him. Fitzpatrick slumped forward and fell across the trail.

An instant later, Hale heard Louis yell: "Look out!"

Molly came around the turn on the run, one pack hanging over the edge, the other brushing the wall, with Louis hanging to the rope, almost being dragged. The mule leaped over Fitzpatrick. Louis stumbled over him and nearly fell, but he was still hanging on when they went out of sight around the next turn.

Hale's legs were shaking when he pulled himself up on the trail. Fitzpatrick was still alive, and he was still trying to get his pistol free. It was under him, or he might have made it. Hale rolled him over and took the weapon.

With death crowding hard, Fitzpatrick mustered a grin. "Hale, you old son-of-a-bitch, you tricked me."

He died just after Louis's voice came back from somewhere down the trail. "It's all right! I've got her stopped!"

Hale went back to get his boots. He found Louis's pistol where he had dropped it at the start of the wild run with Molly. He gathered up the rifles. They seemed to weigh a ton.

He and Louis were both ahead of Molly when they saw Silver Bell far below. "Something's happened down there," Louis mused. "All the tents are gone."

"Too bad." Hale was half asleep on his feet.

Clint Aiken, the liveryman, was waiting for them when they staggered in. "I could tell that Molly mule a mile away. You boys didn't do no good in Spanish Creek, huh?"

"Not much," Hale said. "What kind of a rig have you got for hire?"

"Well, now, I guess I could let you have my light spring wagon, with the little mare.

Ten bucks to Denver. I've got a man there that will bring it back." Aiken watched them lift the pack off Molly. "Holy hell! Don't tell me that's. . . ." He punched his hands against the packs. "Holy hell, holy hell! Everybody here run off to a new camp up the creek!" He looked toward Terrible Pass. "What we need up there is a road."

Before they lifted the packs into the wagon, they weighed them on Aiken's scales. Louis's was fifteen pounds heavier than Hale's.

"Twenty dollars is pretty cheap for the rig," Aiken said. "I really ought to charge more."

Hale gave him a twenty-dollar gold piece.

"Is that what I said?" Aiken sighed. "Well, all right, if that's what I said." He leaned over the wagon box to punch one of the packs again. "One thing about mining, you don't have to bargain and cheat and argue to make a living. You take gold out of the ground and it's clean, honest money, and nobody suffers because you took something away from him. Ain't that a fact?"

"Treat that Molly mule good," Hale said. "I'll be back for her."

Louis stayed in the wagon while Hale went into the store for cheese and crackers and canned tomatoes. They took turns eating and driving. Afterward, with Louis holding the lines, he said: "Maybe I can hold out about an hour, and then I'll show you how to sleep in a bouncing wagon."

Braced in the seat, Hale was already dozing. Louis's voice seemed to come from a great distance. Hale kept seeing Fitzpatrick's face. Maybe Sara was right. Perhaps the man had been mad in his own way. It was a stupid lie to say that anyone could die well; the best he could do was to go without whimpering or denying the life he had lived.

Fitzpatrick had done that, all right.

Hale fell asleep.

ABOUT THE AUTHOR

Steve Frazee was born in Salida, Colorado, and in the decade 1926–1936 he worked in heavy construction and mining in his native state. He also managed to pay his way through Western State College in Gunnison, Colorado, from which in 1937 he graduated with a Bachelor's degree in journalism. The same year he also married. He began making major contributions to the Western pulp magazines with stories set in the American West as well as a number of North-Western tales published in *Adventure.* Few can match his Western novels that are notable for their evocative, lyrical descriptions of the open range and the awesome power of natural forces and their effects on human efforts. *Cry Coyote* (1955) is memorable for its strong female protagonists who actually influence most of the major events and bring about the resolution of the central conflict in this story of wheat growers and expansionist cattlemen. *High Cage* (1957) concerns five miners and a woman snowbound at an isolated gold mine on top of Bulmer Peak in which the twin themes of the lust for gold and the struggle against the savagery of both the elements and human nature interplay with increasing, almost tormented intensity. *Bragg's Fancy Woman* (1966) concerns a free-spirited woman who is able to tame a family of thieves. *Rendezvous* (1958) ranks as one of the finest mountain man books, and *The Way Through the Mountains* (1972) is a major historical novel. Not surprisingly, many of Frazee's novels have become major motion pictures. According to the second edition of *Twentieth Century Western Writers* (1991), a Frazee story is possessed of "flawless characterization, particularly when it involves the clash of human passions; believable dialogue; and the ability to create and sustain damp-palmed suspense."

The employees of Thorndike Press hope you have enjoyed this Large Print book. All our Thorndike, Wheeler, and Kennebec Large Print titles are designed for easy reading, and all our books are made to last. Other Thorndike Press Large Print books are available at your library, through selected bookstores, or directly from us.

For information about titles, please call:
  (800) 223-1244

or visit our Web site at:
  http://gale.cengage.com/thorndike

To share your comments, please write:
  Publisher
  Thorndike Press
  10 Water St., Suite 310
  Waterville, ME 04901